# DROP DEAD DIVA

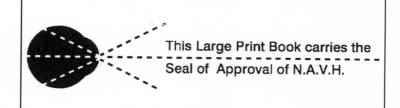

This Large Print Book carries the
Seal of Approval of N.A.V.H.

# Drop Dead Diva

## A SLEUTHING SISTERS MYSTERY

# Christine Lynxwiler, Jan Reynolds, and Sandy Gaskin

**THORNDIKE PRESS**

*A part of Gale, Cengage Learning*

GALE
CENGAGE Learning™

Detroit • New York • San Francisco • New Haven, Conn • Waterville, Maine • London

**GALE**
CENGAGE Learning·

3  1257  01837  7225

Copyright © 2008 by Christine Lynxwiler, Jan Reynolds, and Sandy Gaskin.

Scripture taken from the Holy Bible, New International Version®, NIV®. Copyright © 1973, 1978, 1984 by International Bible Society. Used by permission of Zondervan. All rights reserved.

Thorndike Press, a part of Gale, Cengage Learning.

**LIBRARY OF CONGRESS CATALOGING-IN-PUBLICATION DATA**

Lynxwiler, Christine.
  Drop dead diva : a sleuthing sisters mystery / by Christine Lynxwiler, Jan Reynolds, Sandy Gaskin.
    p. cm. — (Alibis in Arkansas ; bk. 2) (Thorndike Press large print Christian mystery)
    ISBN-13: 978-1-4104-1752-7 (hardcover : alk. paper)
    ISBN-10: 1-4104-1752-2 (hardcover : alk. paper)
    1. Women singers—Crimes against—Fiction. 2. Murder—Investigation—Fiction. 3. Branson (Mo.)—Fiction. 4. Sisters—Fiction. 5. Large type books. I. Reynolds, Jan (Jan Pearle) II. Gaskin, Sandy. III. Title.
  PS3612.Y554D76 2009
  813'.6—dc22                                    2009014485

Published in 2009 by arrangement with Barbour Publishing, Inc.

Printed in the United States of America
1 2 3 4 5 6 7 13 12 11 10 09

To our amazing extended families — in-laws, uncles, aunts, cousins, nieces, and nephews. You're precious to us, and each of you helped shape who we are. Thank you.

And to the friendly people of Branson, Missouri, who make their town our favorite place to vacation!

# 1

A good name is more desirable than great riches; to be esteemed is better than silver or gold.

PROVERBS 22:1

"Who in the world would name a child Holly Wood?" I glanced over at Carly, who was engrossed in her tattered copy of *Holly Wood: The Queen of Country Music.*

*For that matter, who in the world would read Holly's autobiography?* But I wisely kept my hands on the wheel, my eyes on the hills and curves of the highway before us, and that last question to myself. My older sister Carly was a big fan of Holly Wood, country music's female performer of the decade. Especially since Holly was originally from our hometown of Lake View, Arkansas.

Carly looked up from her book and rolled her eyes. "Gracious, Jenna. Everybody knows that story."

7

My mouth twitched at her exaggerated drawl. We were born and raised in Arkansas, and our native language was definitely "Southern." But Carly's decade in the Deep South — Atlanta — apparently made her a master at the art of all things below the Mason-Dixon Line.

"Not everybody, I guess."

She sighed. "When Holly was born, her parents were worried about sibling jealousy, so they let Ruth, her ten-year-old sister, name her."

I snorted. "Brilliant parenting strategy. They probably read about it in some article written by Dr. I-Give-Child-Rearing-Advice-Even-Though-I've-Never-Actually-Had-Kids. Then they thought it was a great idea, until they were stuck with that ridiculous name."

"You know, that could be considered the pot callin' the kettle black. You offer advice about kids in your Dear Pru column all the time."

I cranked up the air-conditioning one notch. She had a point. Taking over the advice column in our small town's local paper had started out as a way for me to gather information in an amateur murder investigation. But after the murder was solved, I'd found myself reluctant to give up the position. So in addition to my day job as manager of the Lake View Athletic Club, I moonlighted as sage advice columnist, Dear Pru. And occasionally I did have to answer questions that dealt with raising children.

"True, but I always confer with you about those letters." I nodded toward the backseat where Carly's preteen twins, Hayley and Rachel, were engrossed in a DVD, and her sixteen-year-old son, Zac, was listening to his MP3 player with his eyes closed. Even though her husband had left her for a stick-figure model when she was pregnant with the twins, as far as I was concerned, Carly had done an amazing job of raising the kids alone. "My own personal parenting expert."

Carly followed my gaze. "Yeah, at least I didn't let any of my kids name each other." She tossed me a sideways grin. "Unfortunately neither did Mama and Daddy. Let's see. I think I was in my Sesame Street stage about the time you were born."

"Oscar the Grouch Stafford? Believe me, I'd have changed it as soon as I was old enough." I crept past the city-limit sign behind a long line of traffic. If Marta hadn't been having her grand opening now, I wouldn't have chosen to make this trip in June, but even now during its peak season,

I liked to think of Branson, Missouri, as the city that's worth the wait.

"But Holly's *sister* named her," Carly protested. "How could she change it?"

I snorted. I didn't buy that sentimentality. "It still amazes me that anybody would — oh, forget it." Talk about wasted breath.

Carly closed her book. "Forget what?"

My sister and I are different in a lot of ways, but neither one of us will ever let a "forget it" slide. So I knew the discussion wasn't over yet. With my hands still on the steering wheel, I shrugged. "You'd think she'd have used marriage as a way out of a bizarre name, but no . . . five marriages later, she's still Holly Wood."

"Actually, she did take Maurice Seaton's last name the first time they were married, but that was before she was famous. After that, her stage manager thought her career had a better chance if she kept Holly Wood, so when she divorced Maurice and married Carl, the stage manager, she went back to —"

"She's what? Thirty-seven or so? And she's been married five times already? Don't you think that's overkill, even for a celebrity?" I wasn't jealous, but I was thirty and hadn't even been married once. There was a minute there on Valentine's Day when I thought

Alex was going to propose, but he was just bending down to tie his shoe. After eight months of dating, I'd finally decided that just as I'd gotten over my commitment issues, he'd apparently developed some.

"Ah, don't be so hard on her, honey," Carly drawled. "She's had a tough time of it. Even back in high school, she was all mixed up. I'm prayin' she'll straighten her life up someday."

Back in high school? Back in high school, Carly had barely been on the same planet as Miss Popularity Holly Wood. When Holly had risen to the top of the social ladder at Lake View High in tenth grade, Carly and her best friend, Marta, were impressionable eighth graders.

I was guessing that Holly figured she already had her life about as "straightened up" as it could go. "Who would have dreamed back then that Marta would open her own theater in Branson and Holly would be the opening act?" How many times over the years when we watched the CMA awards had I heard Carly and Marta brag about saving Holly a seat on the bus every day? Of course, they glossed over the fact that neither of them actually ever got to sit with her. She shooed them away as soon as her size-zero designer jeans slid onto the torn vinyl seat.

"You're right, sugar, nobody saw that one coming. Marta and I had a different dream — *we* wanted to be the opening act." Carly laughed. "Even though I had absolutely no talent whatsoever. I guess every teenage girl wants to be a star."

Everyone but me. I just wanted to swim. As a young Olympic star, the attention came as an unwelcome part of the package.

"So Marta sounded pretty desperate on the phone, huh?"

Carly grunted. "Let's just say that Holly's reputation for being difficult must be justly deserved. I've never heard Marta so rattled." She pointed to a road sign, and I obediently turned. "Or so grateful as when I told her you were taking some vacation days and we could come earlier than we planned."

I held up a hand to shade my eyes from the sun glinting off the Branson Country Paradise Theater. I pulled into the circular drive and parked then smirked. "I hope you told her that I hadn't had a vacation since I started working at the club. Just so I don't look like a total flake."

"No worries. She knows how dependable you are. Thanks for throwing some stuff in a suitcase and coming with me so fast."

"I needed a distraction." I slapped my

hand on the steering wheel and opened my door. "Let's go meet Holly Wood."

The combination hotel/theater was being remodeled, and even though the work was only half done, it was an impressive plantation-style building. John and Marta were convinced this place was the deal of the century. And since they'd invested their life savings in it, I hoped they were right.

"Cool place." Zac took out his earbuds and stuffed them in his pocket as he climbed out of the backseat.

"And it's not even finished yet," I assured him as we all got out and started walking toward the entrance.

"Wow!" Rachel pointed to the giant guitar beside the gate.

"Wow, what?" Hayley asked. "What's so great about Paul Bunyan's guitar?"

The twins are identical and used to enjoy their "alike" status. But lately, although they still got along, they'd been trying to be as different from each other as possible.

"It's huge," Rachel said defensively as they reached the shadow of it.

"Watch out! I think it's falling," Hayley yelled and dodged out of the way.

Rachel jumped then glared at her sister. "Mom!"

"The drama tweens strike again," Zac

13

muttered as he walked past me into the building.

Carly led the way to the door with the Office sign above it. I spotted Marta's dark no-nonsense haircut across the foyer. She had her back to us, arranging a display case of pamphlets.

"Anybody home?" Carly called.

Marta spun around. "Oh, girl, it's so good to see you." She enfolded Carly in a hug, and the twins wrapped their arms around her, too. In spite of her cheery smile, dark circles shaded the area under her eyes. Whatever the Paradise Theatre was offering, a good night's sleep must not have been on the program.

We chatted for a few minutes, carefully avoiding the topic of the headliner act. Finally, Marta motioned toward our bag-laden arms. "Let me show you where you'll be staying." We followed her down a long hallway. "We only have the performer's wing open next to the stage." She glanced back at us and wrinkled her nose. "Holly and her people are taking up most of the available rooms. But we saved one of the larger suites for y'all."

Zac's eyes widened. "Sweet. A suite."

We grinned and Marta glanced at Carly. "No kitchen, though. But we live in a little cottage right behind the Paradise. You can use my kitchen while you're here. I've got it stocked for baking. Just for you."

Carly beamed. "Thanks."

I didn't say anything, but the offer really didn't bode well for our stay. Those of us who know Carly, including Marta, know that she bakes when she gets upset.

Marta unlocked a door. "We aren't opening the rest of the hotel until after the grand opening of the theater. So Holly and her entourage are the only ones here now. And a skeleton staff."

"Thanks for inviting us," I said as we walked into the room, unsure whether she wanted to talk about the reason we were here.

"Oh, don't thank me yet. You'll both earn your keep. That woman has enough demands to keep a small army hopping. You may be sorry you came before it's all over." She hugged us again. "I'm going to leave y'all alone until morning though. We'll get together then and figure out the best plan of attack."

Attack? Sounded like battle lines had been drawn. And she *had* mentioned an army. . . . I let my duffel bag strap slide off my shoulder and put my hands to the small of my back. "Is it okay if I use the pool in the

15

morning?"

Her face fell. "Oh, I'm sorry, Jenna. Our pool isn't ready yet." She brightened. "But I made arrangements for you to swim at the health club down the street. It's just a block away, and they were thrilled to have the great Jenna Stafford as an honored guest." She waved and headed back up to the front office.

Carly dumped her suitcase on the luggage bench. "She means well, Jenna. She just doesn't realize how hard that whole Olympic thing was on you. People who haven't experienced it don't realize fame isn't all it's cracked up to be."

"It's okay." I wished I felt more gracious. It was bad enough that my boss, Bob, had insisted we capitalize on my notoriety as a past Olympic swimmer. But when I wasn't on official business of the Lake View Athletic Club, I tried to forget my brief turn in the spotlight when I was a teen. Maybe if I had a medal to show for it, I'd feel differently. But I'm not sure.

The twins came bursting out of one of the bedrooms. "Awesome room," they sang in chorus and then ran back to their newly discovered play area.

Carly and I shared a look. Simultaneous talking — something we'd always taken for granted with the two of them — hadn't happened much lately. Maybe this trip would restore a little bit of their unique twin-ness.

"Twin beds," I murmured as I glanced in the doorway. "Fitting."

Carly smiled. "Blue and yellow. Their favorite colors. I'll have to thank Marta." She stepped to the door of the second bedroom and motioned to me. Zac was sprawled across the red comforter on his double bed, earbuds stuck in his ears, seemingly dead to the world.

"Is he asleep?" I whispered.

"Who knows?" She closed his door gently. "How about pizza delivered in for supper? Since we're all so tired, I thought we might make it an early night."

"That's the best thing you've said all day."

While we waited for the pizza, we explored the other two rooms. "You can have the one with the Jacuzzi tub in the bathroom," Carly offered. "Since you're part fish."

"I'll take you up on that. But only if you promise to use it any time you want."

"If you're going to twist my arm, then what choice do I have?" she drawled.

Five minutes later, we met back in the spacious living area. Carly settled into an overstuffed rocker and turned back to her book. "Want me to read some of this aloud?

So we'll be better prepared to help?"

I shook my head, probably too quickly. "That's okay. I'll look at it later." Truth was, I'd already learned more about Holly Wood than I'd ever wanted to know. Unless I ended up as a contestant on *Jeopardy!* and she was one of the categories. Which could happen, I guess. At least the part about her being a category.

Thirty minutes later, a knock sounded on the door, and I jumped up to look out the peephole. Instead of the pizza deliveryman, Marta stared back at me.

I yanked the door open. "Come in."

"I know I said I wouldn't bother y'all tonight, but I need a breather. I think I need my head examined." Marta ran her hands through her thick short hair. "Why did I ever dream it would be wonderful having her here?"

"Holly?" Carly asked softly.

"Who else? She's only been here three days and it feels more like three years."

Carly shook her head. "Bless your heart."

I motioned for Marta to sit down. "What can we do?"

"Right now she wants smoked salmon and a salad. John's gone to get it." She shook her head. "You know, he's easygoing, but I don't know how much longer he'll put up

18

with this. As soon as he left, she called me and said she needs a manicurist. Apparently she broke a nail while she was impatiently tapping them on the table, waiting for her food." She grimaced. "Okay, I'm kidding about that. But her nail is broken."

"Glad to see you've still got your sense of humor." Carly patted her on the shoulder. "I think I can fix her nail. I do manicures for the twins and their friends occasionally."

"Thanks." Marta started to push to her feet, but Carly gently shoved her back down.

"Here's a deal for you. You stay here with the kids and wait for our pizza, and Jenna and I will take care of Holly."

I'd have raised an eyebrow if I was able. But that wasn't a talent with which God had blessed me. Almost as if she were reading my mind, though, even without the raised eyebrow, Carly shot me a stern look over her shoulder that said, "We came to help."

Marta leaned her head back against the chair and closed her eyes. "You two are angels in disguise."

Guilt niggled at me. Why couldn't I just be gracious like Carly?

We turned to leave, but Marta called after us. "Wait. You need to wash off your makeup and put your hair up."

"Huh?" Even Carly, Miss I-Know-Every-thing-about-Holly-Wood looked stumped.

Marta shook her head. "Says she's allergic to shampoos and cosmetic smells, except her own. Between us, I think she just doesn't want anyone around who might be competition."

Wordlessly, Carly pulled a bandanna from her makeup bag and tied it around her short dark curls. She dug deeper into the bag, found her makeup remover pads, and started swiping her face.

I opened my mouth to protest, but the pleading look in my sister's eyes silenced me. I secured my long red curls high on top of my head with a bear-claw clip. "I just have moisturizer on; do you think that counts?"

No answer. "Fine. I'll let my skin dry out." I used a washcloth from the bathroom to scrub my face until it tingled.

Out in the hallway, though, I got my voice back. "Can you imagine anyone being so self-centered?" Even my boss's daughter, Lisa, with her ridiculous demands couldn't top this.

Carly was already bouncing along three steps ahead of me, and in spite of Marta's warnings, I was pretty sure she was *excited.*

Sure enough, she looked over her shoulder at me and grinned as wide as a beauty queen. "We're about to see Holly Wood, Jenna. Up close and personal. How can that be a bad thing?"

I remembered the defeated look in Marta's eyes and shuddered at my sister's naïveté. But I forced my feet to keep walking. Someone had to look after Carly in her innocence.

When we reached Holly's suite, I tapped on the door. Carly, never shy, but apparently feeling especially forward at the moment, rattled the handle. As she shoved on the door, it opened. Not latched, I guessed, but the low lights and the shadowy vastness of the interior lent a creepy aura to the place. We stared in the open doorway at the elegant colonial furniture. So this was the Presidential Suite. It made our four-bedroom suite look like a child's playhouse.

"Hello?" Carly called softly into the cavernous room. We took a few steps inside and froze beside the fireplace when we heard a familiar voice.

"It's a disaster and only you can fix it. I need you here now, CeeCee. It's urgent."

Facing the floor-to-ceiling window, Holly, cell phone clutched to her ear, was holding her offending nail up to the light, apparently calling her own personal manicurist. Her signature blond curls cascaded halfway down her back. "Saturday? I can't wait that long."

As if she sensed our presence, Holly spun around. Whoa. The last time I saw a top that tight and short was when I pulled a dry-clean-only sweater from the dryer. Even then I hadn't thought to pair it with an elegant silver-hoop belly-button ring. Another missed opportunity. Or not.

Holly's perfect features broke into a scowl, and she spoke quickly into the phone. "Fine. I've got to go. Come by as soon as you get into town." She flipped the phone shut and glared at us. "Who are you and what are you doing in here?"

# 2

For the lips of an adulteress drip honey,
and her speech is smoother than oil.
PROVERBS 5:3

I stepped forward. "I'm Jenna Stafford. No relation to Jim." I couldn't count the number of times I'd been asked in Branson if I was related to funny guy Jim Stafford. But judging from Holly's answering grunt, she wasn't wondering anyway. I rushed on. "We're here to help with your fingernails. You remember my sister, Carly. From Lake View High School."

I was hoping my phrasing would save Carly any embarrassment if Holly didn't remember her. But Carly grinned. "Don't be silly, Jenna. I'm sure she doesn't remember me. She's met so many people since then."

"But when someone saves you a seat on the bus every day, it seems to me like that should forever imprint her in your memory," I deadpanned. Maybe it's my near brush with being one, but something about celebrities makes me slightly irreverent of their status.

Carly glared at me. But before she could give me a piece of her mind, Holly pasted on a smile as artificial as her, um . . . fingernails . . . and floated toward my sister. "Of course I remember you, darling. . . ." She stretched out her hand.

"Carly," I supplied, just in case.

"Carly," Holly repeated and waved toward the other room. "Now be a dear and fetch my emergency nail kit from the dresser."

Carly had been about to take Holly's hand, but she realized her faux pas in time and jerked her own back. "Okay." She hurried out, and in just a few seconds she was back with a little white kit. "Want me to give you a whole manicure? Or will your own manicurist be arriving soon?"

"My own manicurist?" Holly's voice had a naturally haughty tone, sort of like a spoiled child. Condescending.

"CeeCee?" I reminded her. Apparently my role in this little production was to fill in the blanks in her memory when it came to names.

"CeeCee?" she repeated. Then she

24

laughed. "CeeCee does many things for me, but nails are not among them."

"Oh, sorry," Carly muttered. "We just thought . . ."

"Yes, well, eavesdropping is never a good idea, is it?"

"Right. Sorry." Carly's embarrassment and apology annoyed me. I'd had enough.

"Look, we just came to help you. If you don't want our help, we'll be happy to leave." I didn't want to be snippy, but it had only been twelve hours since I escaped from one demanding diva, and I wasn't ready to go back to being bossed around by another one. I guess Holly realized I meant it, because she backed down.

"No, of course I don't want you to leave." Her smile would have melted butter. "Please fix my broken nail." She waved her hand in Carly's face. The glitter of her rings nearly blinded me. "I keep them short to play the guitar, but they're still important to me."

As she and Carly sat on the elegant sofa, I wandered around the room and listened to their muted conversation as I examined an arrangement of framed photos on the end table. Most of the photos were of Holly receiving awards. I had to admit she was a gorgeous woman with her perfect figure, beautiful smile, and glorious hair.

"You have no idea how hard it is to be in the spotlight all the time, Carly. My fans are everywhere." Holly sounded tearful. "I'm even afraid to go out to eat for fear of being mobbed."

Poor girl. Probably cried all the way to the bank. But sucker Carly was buying every word. I guess my experience with my boss's daughter, Lisa — aka prima donna and the sole reason I was in desperate need of a vacation — had made me just a little bit cynical. Okay, a lot jaded probably.

"My husband, Buck, has been a rock, though. He's wonderful," Holly gushed. "He's so tolerant of the paparazzi and has even agreed to do some interviews."

"Is he here?" Carly carefully applied clear polish to Holly's nail.

"He's my personal trainer, too, so he's probably at the gym working out. Ruth's around somewhere, but she's never in here when I need her."

Carly made a noncommittal sound in reply and put the brush back into the bottle then closed it.

"I let my personal assistant have a vacation while I came here. I knew Marta would take care of me." Then her tone switched to petulant. "But she's been so busy with this place, that she . . ." She looked at us as if weighing her words. "Well, let's just say, it's a good thing you came to help me or I don't know what I'd have done."

Oh, boohoo. I didn't know how much longer I could stomach this. If it weren't for Marta, I would have just told Holly to fix her own nail and then gone for a swim.

But my sweet sister smiled and patted Holly's hand before releasing it. "I know we'll enjoy being here. I can't wait for the show Friday night." Carly stood and I headed for the door. Just as I reached for the knob, a dour-faced woman pushed it open. She had her arms full of clothes, and without a word, she walked past me and headed for the bedroom. As Carly shut the door behind us, we could hear their raised voices.

Carly glanced behind us. "That's Ruth, Holly's older sister."

"Sounds like she's a little irritated."

"Probably just something to do with the show. She takes care of Holly's wardrobe and makeup."

"Oh, as opposed to her vacationing personal assistant, who takes care of everything else." Oops. Was my disdain showing?

Carly smiled. "Right."

Was there anything my sister didn't know about the Queen of Country? I opened my mouth to suggest she try out for *Jeopardy!,* but my cell phone rang before I got the words out. I glanced at the caller ID. Apparently Alex finally remembered my number.

"Hey there, water girl."

Even after all these months, his deep voice still made my heartbeat accelerate. "Hey."

"How's it feel to be hanging out with the stars?"

I smiled into the phone. If he only knew. "Tiring."

"Running from the paparazzi?"

"Something like that. How's work?"

"It's going great. But I was thinking of coming up there this weekend."

Stop the presses. Considering he'd worked every Saturday for the last month and a half, this was big news.

"To Branson?"

"Unless you're really in Vegas. Yes, Branson."

I laughed. "Well, yeah. Can you really come?" He'd been working so hard for the last two weeks, I'd barely seen him even before I left town.

"If it's okay with you, I'll try. I miss you, Jenna."

"I miss you, too."

We chatted a few more minutes, but when

we hung up, my mind wandered back to his unabashed confession — he missed me. And he was willing to drive several hours to see me. Maybe his commitment issues were working themselves out.

The next morning, I left Carly and the kids sleeping and slipped out to the breakfast area to get us something to eat. While I was surveying the continental spread, a blond hunk sauntered in. He scanned the room, and his gaze settled on me. All over me, actually. Ick.

He sauntered over with a wolfish grin and stuck out his hand. "You must be one of Marta's friends. I'm Buck Fisher."

Holly's earlier gushing came back to me. Buck Fisher. Holly's personal trainer and husband. An unexpected pang of pity for the diva hit me.

"Jenna Stafford." I returned his greeting then tried to figure out how to extricate my hand without yanking it away.

"Any relation to Jim?" He grinned big, clearly getting quite a kick out of his little joke.

I was tempted to say, "As a matter of fact . . ." but thought better of it. Those kinds of lies always come back to bite one on the proverbial behind. "No." Abrupt answer, but I had a feeling I'd better not encourage this guy or I'd be fighting off his massive hands every time I was near him.

I glanced over Buck's shoulder, trying to avoid his roving eyes. A beautiful girl with long black hair and flashing green eyes was headed toward us, and it didn't look like food was on her mind. I recognized her from the posters as Reagan Curtis, Holly's opening act. "Buck."

He dropped my hand and whirled around.

I wiped my palm on my pant leg. It looked like things could get ugly, but I was just grateful for the interruption.

"I've been looking all over for you." Her voice was possessive, and she ignored me completely as she wrapped her long silver fingernails around his arm. "I need breakfast."

*Guess I'm wrong about food not being on her mind,* I thought facetiously.

Buck gave me a quick wink and followed her out the door. Apparently they breakfasted elsewhere.

I loaded a tray and slipped back into our suite, where silence greeted me. I ate a couple of orange slices and grabbed a swimsuit. I could easily be back before they knew I was gone. If not, they'd forgive me once they found the food.

When I pushed open the double doors to the health club, I immediately felt at home. The zip code might be different, but the slight smell of chlorine in the air remained the same. And I loved it. I had the pool all to myself, which was even better.

In the locker room, I changed into my swimsuit and twisted my long curls up into a tight bun. Just like always, I couldn't wait to get in the water.

Halfway through my swimming routine, the door opened and a tall, muscular man came in. His black hair included almost as much salt as pepper, but his dark eyes were sharp as he glanced at me. Just as quickly as he noticed me, he ignored me and dove into the pool. His long arms sliced through the water with ease as he rapidly swam several laps.

From all my years of training, and more recently my job at the health club, I've grown spoiled to swimming alone. But this guy swam with a precision that was a pleasure to watch. When he took a breather, I nodded. "Nice form."

"Thanks," he grunted then dove back in.

I climbed out and slid a towel around me then hurried to the women's shower. When I finished and dressed, I came back out just as the dark-eyed man was reaching for a towel.

"Do you swim professionally?" he asked.

"I might ask you the same thing."

He shook his head. "Exercise only for me."

I hesitated. "Me, too." Which was totally true. And I wasn't ready to dredge up the agony of my Olympic defeat. Certainly not for a total stranger.

"Really? You've never had professional training?"

His hawk nose was distinctive, but his eyes were what grabbed my attention. They seemed to pierce to the marrow to get the facts.

"When I was younger . . ." I found myself saying, then stopped. I heaved my swim bag onto my shoulder and spun on my heel. The faster I got away from this man who seemed to demand the truth the better.

Out on the street, I headed back to the suite, unsure what it was about Hawk Man that had upset me so much. Once I reached our hallway, a door nearby opened, and muted voices drifted toward me. I instinctively glanced over just in time to see Buck step out. Reagan, wearing a short white silk robe, was framed behind him in the doorway.

Buck's smile faded as soon as he saw me.

He glanced back over his shoulder where Reagan stood frozen.

"This isn't what it looks like." He jerked his head toward the door. "She just spilled juice on her clothes."

"Believe me, if you're Marta's friend, you're better off not mentioning this," Reagan piped up. "If Holly gets upset, the show *won't* go on."

Buck shot her a glare then hurried away.

Carly might claim that I'm never at a loss for words, but even Dear Pru didn't know the proper etiquette for a situation such as this. Before I had time to think of something to say, though, my cell phone rang.

I didn't even glance at the caller ID. Anything would be better than this. Reagan took the opportunity to slam the door, so apparently she agreed.

"Hello?"

"Jenna! How's Branson?"

"Bob?" I'd noticed a missed call from my boss, but I'd been in no hurry to return it.

His hearty laugh sounded forced. "Forgot me so soon? Girl, I'm hoping you're about done with vacation and ready to get back to work."

I stopped and leaned against the wall. Considering what I'd been putting up with from his daughter-turned-manager, he should be glad I was taking vacation days and not permanently quitting. "I'm sure Lisa can handle things. After all, you put her in charge, right?"

"Lisa misses you terribly."

I closed my eyes. That was reaching, even for Bob. "Explain to me again how I went from being just about to buy your business — a promise you've been making to me for a long time, I might add — to waiting on your daughter hand and foot while she pretends to do my job."

"She's been through so much with her marriage troubles. I just wanted you to help her get her self-esteem back."

Lisa and her husband had split, and she'd moved back to town a few months ago. Now Bob and Wilma couldn't do enough for their spoiled daughter. Which was exactly why I'd come to hate my job. Lisa had her daddy wrapped around her finger, and Bob was in denial. I'd tried to quit numerous times, but I always felt too sorry for him to go through with it. But if something didn't give, I'd forever be fetching juice drinks for the spoiled socialite and working long hours to fix her mistakes. It was time for Bob to get a taste of Lisa's management skills without me. "Like I told you, I'll be back in two weeks."

I hit the END button before he could reply. Holly and I had something in common. We were both being deceived, and our hopes and dreams lay in the balance.

When I opened the door, the girls were bouncing up and down with excitement. "Zac and Danielle are taking us to Whitewater!" they chorused.

"Good." I had a feeling that for once Zac would be glad to have his sisters along. He'd been friends with John and Marta's daughter his whole life, but now that they were teens, I'd noticed an awkward silence in the air between them.

Carly and I tag-teamed the kids with warnings about not talking to strangers, looking both ways before crossing the street, and my personal contribution, probably because of my red hair and tendency to freckle — wearing sunblock.

When they were gone, I filled Carly in on my phone conversation with Bob. After she sympathized, I told her about Buck and Reagan's hallway drama.

She shook her head. "Like Mama says, 'Life gets so messed up when people throw out their Bibles.' "

Guilt hit me in the gut. I'd started a study of Proverbs a few weeks ago. But lately, with things so bad at the athletic club and Alex breaking our dates in order to work, I'd gotten distracted. Instead of turning to God, I'd been trying to handle it all myself. No wonder my prayers felt like they weren't going above the ceiling these days.

So when Carly left to check in with Marta, I dug out my Bible and spent a little time catching up. By the time Carly came back with our marching orders, I felt like God and I were on speaking terms again.

My newfound pity for Holly made me more understanding as Carly and I played servant all day. Midafternoon, Marta caught us in the hall. "You girls take the rest of the day off. Let your hair down. You deserve it."

I grinned. "In that case, the red roof is calling my name. And the blue one is echoing it." That's another thing I love about Branson. With their brightly colored roofs, its malls are easy to find. "I'm going to get a quick shower and shop 'til I drop." I glanced over at Carly. "How about it?"

She shrugged. "If it's okay with you, I think I'll just stay and help Marta."

I couldn't imagine why anyone would prefer waiting on Holly hand and foot to Branson's terrific outlet malls, but I was just glad she didn't ask me to stay, too.

I returned to the hotel tired and hungry but

halfway done with my Christmas shopping — and it wasn't even July yet. While I was gloating over my finds, Carly stumbled in and collapsed on the bed.

She moaned, bandanna askew and eyes closed.

"What happened to you?"

"Can't walk. Can't talk. Too tired," she mumbled.

Poor girl. I offered to get dinner for us all — or to take the kids out and bring Carly a plate. But she dozed off while we were discussing it.

When the kids bounced in a few minutes later, slightly sunburned — in spite of all my sunblock warnings — and more than slightly filthy, I made an executive decision. They stayed in and washed up, and I made a run for ribs, one of my favorite Branson foods. After everyone was showered, Danielle came back to join us for our feast in the room. When we finished eating, Carly stretched out on the couch with a blanket and pillow. Zac looked at me. "Is it okay if we put a movie in?"

Carly snored softly. I nodded. "Sure, if you keep the volume low."

Dani and Zac pulled their chairs up toward the TV.

The twins followed me into my room. And

while I got ready for bed, they regaled me with drama-filled stories of getting lost and nearly drowning at Whitewater. So ended another day in Paradise.

# 3

Pride goes before destruction, a haughty
spirit before a fall.

PROVERBS 16:18

When Alex called midafternoon Friday and said he had to work after all, I felt like having a prima-donna fit myself. After two days of observing an expert, I was pretty sure I could pull it off. But there was room for only one diva at the Paradise. Maybe if I'd told Alex that for the second day in a row I'd met a mysterious man for a swim, he'd have come anyway. But the way I figured it, we were a little old for silly games. Besides, Hawk Man had totally ignored me this morning, and I'd returned the favor.

So I squashed down my disappointment and ran to the nearest grocery store to get Holly some more Evian. She dismissed us around five, and Carly and I hurried back to the room to shower and dress for the show. Thankfully it didn't take us long to get ready. John called an hour before show time and begged us to go to Holly's dressing room to stop a shouting match that Marta couldn't handle.

"Fine, but I'm not messing with my face or hair," I muttered.

To my surprise, Carly nodded. "Me neither."

As we rounded the corner to Holly's dressing room, we could hear Holly screaming through the closed door. We almost bumped into a guy Marta had introduced to us earlier as Joey from the band. In his midtwenties, "Joey from the band" looked like he wished he were "Joey on another planet." He shrugged and shook his head then brushed past us.

Carly tapped on the door, but when no one answered, she pushed it open. We walked in to see Holly shaking her finger at her sister.

"You deliberately made this smaller so it won't fit me. You'd better quit trying to make me look bad and remember who supports you."

Holly's blue-sequined dress did look like it had been glued onto her. But I wasn't sure it looked any tighter than her normal attire.

Ruth shrugged. "Maybe you should train more and eat less. Assuming your trainer is willing to spend time training you instead of . . ." Ruth clamped her lips together at this interesting juncture. I knew what she was implying, but did Holly?

Carly managed to get the brush out of Holly's hand before she threw it, but it was a close call. My amazing sister even convinced Ruth to let out a seam so the dress would fit. But as Ruth left with the dress, she leveled a look at Holly I would never give my sister. Or anyone else. Holly didn't appear to notice. Instead, she turned her attention to another offender.

"You sneaky, ungrateful beast." Holly's voice was shrill, and I spun around, ready to attack if she was talking to Carly.

Buck filled the doorway, an embarrassed grin playing across his handsome face. She heaved a shoe at his head. Fortunately, or maybe unfortunately, she missed. "Now, Hol . . ."

"Don't you 'Hol' me. I keep you in the lap of luxury and this is how you repay me?"

He nodded at Carly and me. "Preshow nerves." But he backed out with his hands up to ward off any more tossed items. Apparently he'd been this route before.

"That's right. Get out! No one understands me!" She turned on us. "I just want to be alone. Is that too much to ask?" An almost tangible relief washed over the room. Marta mumbled an excuse and sprinted out as if she'd been practicing for the hundred-yard dash. Carly and I didn't exactly linger, either.

But we hadn't been in our room too long before Carly's cell phone rang. She looked at me, cringing.

"Surely you didn't give her your number?"

"Hi, Holly." Carly listened to the frantic voice even I could hear.

"Carly, can you come back? I just go a little crazy before a show."

Carly murmured a soothing "yes" and shut the phone. "Go ahead and shoot me, but I'm going to go back."

For some reason, Carly had decided it was her Christian duty to be there for Holly. I most certainly didn't share her mission, but I couldn't stand to send her into the lion's den alone. "Wait, I'll go with you. You may need me as a shield in case she starts throwing things again."

Holly was pacing in her room when we entered, but she was alone. The offending dress fit beautifully.

"You look great, Holly." I heard the relief in Carly's voice.

Holly snorted. "Naturally, the dress looks fine now that my so-called *sister* fixed it back to normal size."

"Is there somethin' else we can do for you before the show?" Carly asked.

"Bring me a glass of cold water. And I need a throat lozenge from the bag on the dressing table." Poor Holly had nearly had to pour her own water. Good thing we'd gotten there in time. Carly patiently handed her water and unwrapped a lozenge.

"Anything else?"

*Yeah, should we breathe for you?* But Holly inclined her head graciously.

"No, I really must be alone now. I have to get centered before I go onstage so that I can give my all to my fans. Do you realize that some of these poor people have waited years and seeing me in person is their lifelong dream?"

I felt my eyebrows shoot up into my hairline. Did she really believe that?

She sat down at the dressing table and examined her face in the mirror. "It's such a responsibility. Sometimes it's almost too much even for me." She smoothed an imaginary wrinkle. "My one unbreakable rule is that no one enters my dressing room for the thirty minutes before I go onstage. I delve deep into myself and get my psyche ready so I can pour my whole being into my performance."

Okay. We got it. Her whole self and psyche had to get ready so she could fulfill the lifelong dream of her fans. Could we go now? Carly must have been reading my mind again because she nodded and pushed me toward the door.

"We'll see you after the show, Holly. Break a leg."

*Now there's an idea.*

In the hall, I turned to Carly. "Can you believe the total conceit of that woman? 'Back off, lowly one. My one unbreakable rule is that none of the peasants get near me without express permission. It's bad for my delicate psyche.' "

"She doesn't realize how she sounds."

"More than likely, she doesn't care," I whispered as we entered the packed auditorium where Reagan was already in the middle of a song. The audience clapped along with her, but I got the feeling they were waiting for the main event. I glanced around the crowded room. Was Holly right? Had some people waited forever to see her in person? That crossed the line from fan to fanatic in my book.

When Reagan and her band finished, I had to admit that even though she didn't seem to have much in the way of morals, she had talent and a certain amount of stage presence. Apparently the audience agreed, or at least some of them. During the fifteen-minute intermission, she lingered in front of the stage signing autographs.

When the emcee announced Holly and she walked out, the crowd went wild. She offered a self-effacing smile and drawled, "Well, hello, y'all. It's great to be in Branson." People screamed and stomped their feet. Holly glowed. No other word for it. She seemed likeable, even to me, and I knew better.

After the show, Holly, gracious smile still intact, signed autographs for several minutes. Once the crowd dispersed, Carly dragged me over with her to tell Holly how much we enjoyed the show.

Reagan appeared behind us. "Did you notice how much the audience loved my opening number?" she said loudly. "I had to pull back a little after that to keep from stealing the show."

As I remembered Buck leaving Reagan's hotel room, I couldn't keep quiet. "I don't think the crowd needed much encouragement to adore Holly." I couldn't believe I was defending the honor of the most hateful, shallow person I'd met in years.

Holly ignored Reagan.

Reagan shrugged. "Well, they were mostly senior citizens. More her age group."

Carly gasped, but again, Holly seemed not to hear the venomous words. Maybe her psyche was still centered. Or maybe she recognized Reagan's jealousy for what it was.

Out in the hall, Marta turned to us, excitement shining on her tired face. "A sold-out show! Can you believe it? What a grand opening!"

Carly hugged her. "We're so happy for you."

"We couldn't have done it without you both. Let's get the kids and go somewhere and celebrate."

Carly nodded, and I smiled. "I've got some work I need to do back in the room. I'll have to count on Carly to bring me a doggy bag."

"You got it."

After they had collected the kids from the room and were gone, I settled in at the computer. I had an agreement with my editor — I could stay away as long as I stayed on the job, so to speak. I snagged three Dear Pru letters from the stack I'd brought with me and began typing away. Before I fell asleep at the wheel — or in this case, keyboard — I managed to answer all three with a modicum of good sense. As I drifted off to sleep, though, I wondered if I was a little too vehement in my response to the woman who suspected her husband of cheating. While I was advising her to find out the truth at all costs, a picture of Buck and Reagan flashed across my mind.

I swam thirty minutes earlier Saturday morning and avoided Hawk Man. When I got back, Marta insisted Carly and I take the kids to Silver Dollar City. We invited Danielle and enjoyed a few carefree hours scaring ourselves silly on rides like Wildfire and Powder Keg. But by midafternoon the kids were so tired they didn't even argue when Carly said we needed to get back to the hotel.

At the suite, I came out towel drying my hair to find Carly already dressed and relaxing in the recliner.

"Want me to find John and Marta and see if they want to eat with us?"

"Sure." Carly was nearly asleep, so I left her to grab a few minutes' slumber and headed down the hall. I hadn't taken three steps away from the door when my cell rang. I flipped it open. "Did you change your mind about supper?"

47

"Jenna? What are you talking about? Are you girls okay?"

"Mama. We're fine. I'm sorry. I thought you were someone else. How are you and Dad?"

"He's a little grouchy, but I think that's just because he's worried about you suddenly deciding to take vacation days then hightailing it out of town with your sister and the kids."

"Things haven't been good at the club lately." Which she knew but refused to acknowledge. "Tell Dad not to worry. My job will still be waiting for me when I get back." *If I want it.*

"That's what Alex said. Your dad talked to him at breakfast yesterday. Honey, I don't mean to pry, but do you think it's wise to go off for so long and leave Alex here?" She made it sound like I forgot to pack him when I was loading my suitcase.

How wide could one generation gap get? "Alex is a grown man, Mama. If he wants to come to Branson, he's perfectly capable of getting here. I have let him know he's welcome." But he'd let me know he had to work. "What else can I do? Go back home and drag him here?" My voice might have risen a little as I finished that question. I know my blood pressure did.

"You don't have to get huffy."

She was right. They don't call something a "sore" subject for no reason. "I'm sorry. It's just that this is one of those issues Alex has to work out for himself. He knows how I feel. Now the ball's in his court. Besides, you know what they say about absence making the heart grow fonder."

"They also say absence makes the heart go wander." Job's Old Testament friends could take lessons from my mother. "Jenna, darling, I don't want you to be *forward* or anything. But you *can* be subtle about it."

Apparently she heard what she said and remembered who she was talking to. "On second thought, maybe your dad will kind of feel him out and see how he responds. No use risking embarrassment."

"Mama." I wasn't shouting. Exactly. Okay. Maybe I was. But I was thirty years old and my mother was offering to have my dad ask my boyfriend if his intentions were honorable. "Please — do — not — tell — daddy — to — ask — Alex — anything."

"Jenna Stafford, don't use that tone of voice with me." I felt fifteen again. Only I was not the one Mama talked to like that usually. Carly had been the wild child in our family.

"I'm sorry. Really I am. But I was serious

about not wanting Dad to mention me to Alex."

"Okay, honey. You're right. This is between the two of you. I just want you to be happy."

My irritation melted away. I knew she meant it. Sometimes it was just hard to remember that fact when she started trying to work things out for me.

"I *am* happy. I have a great family. If I end up marrying Alex, fine. If not, then God must have something else in mind." I sounded so trusting. Maybe if I said it out loud often enough, I'd really feel that way.

"That's the right attitude, sweetie. Tell Carly and the kids hello for me. I'll call Carly when I get a chance. The cabins are full right now." My parents own resort cabins, and I know from experience that when Stafford Cabins are full, Mama has little time for anything else. "Oh, and of all things, Harvey says he and Alice are very serious about selling the diner or quitting business altogether. If they do that, what will our guests do?"

I started to remind her that there were other places to eat in town, but then I realized she'd transferred her worry to something besides me. Without waiting for an answer, she finished with, "Your daddy just came in. Take care. Love you."

"You, too. I've got to go find Marta —" I started to say, but I was talking to dead air.

A few seconds later, I found Marta without any trouble but immediately wished I hadn't.

"You can't do this to me!" Marta's voice escalated to a near scream, drawing me toward Holly's suite. "We've invested everything in this hotel. You'll ruin us!"

"Oh, come on, Marta. Grow up. I can do whatever I want. I'm the star, remember?"

"Grow up? That's a joke coming from you. You're still as self-centered as you were when we were in school. You haven't grown up at all."

"Me?" Holly's mocking laugh chilled me. "You're still a groupie just like you were in junior high."

"You signed a contract." Marta sounded rather desperate now.

"With an exemptive clause about illness." Holly's voice took on a saccharine quality. "I really can't help it if I develop a bad migraine. And I won't perform if I can't give my best to my adoring fans."

I glanced behind me. Should I go back to our suite? Or try to rescue Marta?

"So help me, Holly, you will be on that stage when the curtain goes up, or . . ." Marta's voice was as tight as clenched fists.

Holly's voice turned hard. "You'd better leave now."

As the doorknob turned, I impulsively ducked into the janitor's closet across the hall. I stood there, surrounded by mops and brooms, my heart pounding, until all was quiet then returned to our room without trying to follow Marta. I woke Carly and told her what I'd heard and that I didn't end up asking the Hills to eat with us. I motioned toward the kids, glued to a movie. "Hey, let's fling the kids a purse of gold and let them pick up dinner. We'll feel a lot better after we eat."

"Sounds like a plan."

"Here, slaves. Earn your keep." I waved several bills in front of them to get their attention. It worked. Kids are so easy.

A little while later, Carly's cell phone pealed out the first few bars of Holly's first number-one hit, aptly titled "What's Wrong with Me Is You." My sentiments exactly.

"Calm down, Holly. Jenna and I will be right there." Carly flipped the phone shut and hustled me out of the room. Before we knew it, we were in The Presence again. And the Country Queen was not pleased. Surprise.

"Reagan had better be out of the main auditorium when I'm introduced tonight or she'll be sorry. She hung around signing autographs last night, trying to upstage me. If it happens again, Buck will have to remove her using all the force he needs to." I smothered the thought that neither Buck nor Reagan would probably consider that punishment. "That is, if Buck happens to appear for the show. Who knows where he's been all day?"

I knew it was a rhetorical question, but I could have offered an educated guess.

"If he knows what's good for him, he'll remember that airtight prenup—" She stopped as if she just realized we were still there. "I hope Ruth didn't mess up my dress for tonight."

"You looked great last night, and I'm sure you'll look even better tonight." This from Carly — the pourer-of-oil-on-troubled-waters.

"Yes, well, not if you all stay here and gab all night."

I almost laughed out loud at the pointed look Holly gave us. Had she forgotten that she called us here? I shook my head as Carly and I made our way back down to our room. Considering the show was supposed to be starting immediately, we were the ones in danger of not getting any supper, thanks to Holly's summons.

"I'd rather miss part of Reagan's performance than not eat," Carly said, as if she read my mind.

"Me, too." I opened the suite door and hurried in. "I thought the kids would have been back by now."

The words were barely out of my mouth when they burst in, bringing with them the wonderful aroma of burgers hot off the Mc-griddle.

While we ate, the twins launched into a tale about almost getting run over in the hotel parking lot. Zac shrugged. "They ran ahead of me, and some guy squealed his tires braking for them to walk by. He stopped in plenty of time, though. No big deal."

When Carly didn't scold the kids for running in the parking lot, I glanced over at her. She was staring off into space. "Carly? You okay?"

She gave me a rueful grin. "I feel guilty that we weren't there earlier to calm Holly. What if she ruins things for Marta tonight?"

"Look how well she did last night once she got onstage. And she seemed okay just now. It's all going to be fine." I dipped my last french fry in Ranch dressing and popped it into my mouth.

Carly reminded the kids not to leave the

suite or let anyone in. We opened the door and followed the sound of blaring music the short distance to the auditorium entrance. We handed our tickets to the usher and walked in just as Reagan belted out the last line of a classic woman-done-wrong song.

When we were seated, I glanced at the aisle directly beside my seat. How hard would it be to slip out to see the Presleys or Yakov Smirnoff and make it back before anyone realized I was gone? A laugh would have been nice. Wishful thinking. Maybe Marta would let us come back sometime when she had a comedian headliner.

A low-maintenance comedian headliner.

A few minutes later, Carly leaned over to me. "She's more nervous than she was last night."

I nodded.

Reagan finished out the set with professionalism, if not pizzazz. When she sang the last notes of her closing song, she exited the stage to polite applause. And she didn't appear to sign autographs, so Holly must have gotten her point across.

A minute or two later, a disembodied voice proclaimed, "Ladies and gentlemen, please welcome to the Paradise Theater stage . . . Holly Wood!"

The lights flashed up and down, the drums rolled, and — nothing. No Holly. The audience went wild. After several minutes of cheering finally subsided to loud complaints, the emcee cleared his throat and tried again. "Ladies and gentlemen, direct from sold-out performances all over the USA, greet four-time CMA Entertainer of the Year, Ms. Holly Wood!"

The audience erupted into even louder cheers, but Holly still didn't show.

"Ladies and Gentlemen . . ." The emcee was definitely nervous himself by now and apparently taking direction from someone backstage. "Holly has been delayed, but Reagan Curtis will sing one more number while we're waiting."

I turned to Carly in horror. "Do you think Holly decided to show Marta she meant what she said about not showing up?"

Carly shrugged. "When we left her, she sure sounded like she was planning to sing tonight, so I don't know."

Reagan bounced back out, a little disheveled, but all smiles. "Just remember, anything worth having is worth waiting for." The audience twittered, and she launched into a cheerful upbeat song.

Marta hurried down the aisle toward us. She leaned across me and hissed, "Carly, would you go get Holly, please? I'll stay here in case we need crowd control, but hurry."

I put my hand on Carly's arm. "I'll do it. I may not be Gandhi, but I can keep peace when it's necessary. Be right back."

Like the athlete I used to be, I fairly sprinted down front and flashed my back-stage pass at the row of security guards. Once in the hall, I made a beeline to Holly's dressing room and knocked lightly. If her psyche wasn't centered by now, she'd just have to go onstage and take her chances. Taking a deep breath, I opened the door. Holly — decked out for the show — was almost reclining in her chair in front of her mirror.

"Holly, you're late! You've missed your cue. Hur—" I broke off as nausea slammed into my gut.

Holly's unfocused eyes were bulging in a blue face.

# 4

The righteousness of the blameless
makes a straight way for them, but
the wicked are brought down
by their own wickedness.
PROVERBS 11:5

I've never seen anyone look so . . . blue. A slender plastic thread was draped across Holly's neck and down the front of her red bangled dress. I quickly averted my gaze to her hands. At least they were normal color.

Even though I knew she was dead by her eyes, I touched her wrist to feel for a pulse. The fingernail Carly had fixed was broken again. Holly would have a thing or two to say to my sister about that, no doubt. Except she wouldn't be able to speak. Not with her face blue like that. My feet felt like lead bricks, and hysteria bubbled up in my throat. There was no pulse.

I clutched my stomach and bolted from the room. Which way? The stage area or the private section? Maybe I wasn't as calm as I should be. The decision was taken from me when Buck turned the corner coming from the suite hallway. Before I could say anything, he accosted me. "They said Holly's not onstage. Have you seen her?"

Boy! Had I ever. I stifled a nervous sob. "She — she's — call 911."

"What?" He looked at me like I was crazy and reached for the doorknob. "Holly?"

He had the door opened a scant inch when I finally came to my senses. I pulled it shut and grabbed his arm.

"Buck," I said, fast and low. "Holly's dead."

"Wha — ? Is this a joke?" Buck must have seen the truth in my face. He backed up uncertainly. "Are you sure? Maybe we can help her."

I shuddered as I remembered her face. "I'm sorry. She's definitely dead. We need the police." I dialed 911 on my cell and pulled Buck toward the nearest security guard.

The tall blond guard looked at me as if I were crazy as I babbled to him and the 911 operator at the same time. His partner, older and obviously more experienced, took my cell phone and barked out a clear assessment of the situation. When he finished the call, he narrowed his eyes and put a seemingly friendly hand on Buck's arm. "Why don't you go with us to check this out?"

Buck frowned but nodded. They started down the hall to Holly's room, and the older guard looked back at me. "Be sure you're available to talk to the police when they get here."

I nodded numbly and walked into the auditorium. A faint buzzing echoed in my ears, but I was pretty sure that was shock. Could someone be in shock and know it? I surveyed the scene, trying to get my bearings.

Reagan was up on the stage, singing her heart out to a restless audience. Marta came scurrying down the aisle, with John right on her heels. "Where's Holly?"

I motioned to the double doors, and we stepped outside, where I broke the news as gently as possible.

"I don't believe it," Marta said, but the tears that spilled down her cheeks said otherwise. John wrapped his arm around her shoulders.

She looked up at him. "We have to go see what's going on."

He nodded, and they left, whispering furiously.

I watched them go and then glanced down at the marble-tiled floor of the lobby. If I could just rest for a while, I'd feel better. The double doors opened behind me and Carly stepped out. "Jenna? What's wrong? You look awful."

I nodded. "Awful."

She put her arm around me. "Honey, what happened?"

The sympathetic tone in her voice melted the wall I'd erected when I found the body. Hot tears splashed onto my cheeks.

She eased me over to a bench and helped me sit down, then sat beside me. "Tell me."

When I finished, she gasped. "You poor thing."

I cried for a few minutes while she patted my shoulder. Then I sat up straight and swiped my eyes. "Poor Holly."

"Yes, poor Holly. A person can only make so many enemies without making the wrong one." In spite of her matter-of-fact tone, I could see her own eyes were moist with tears.

"I'm sorry." I slipped my hand into hers and squeezed. "I know you really cared about her."

She nodded. "I did. I thought I could

make a difference."

"You gave it your best shot, Carly."

"Who do you think murdered her?" Carly whispered and glanced back at the double doors, where we could still hear Reagan singing.

I shrugged. "She had even more enemies than Hank did."

For a few seconds, we didn't speak, remembering, I'm sure, the horrible murder of the newspaper editor in our hometown a few months ago. Zac had been a suspect, and Carly and I had eventually solved the murder, but we'd almost gotten ourselves killed in the process.

"Promise me something," Carly said softly.

I looked over at her. "What?"

"We're going to stay out of this murder investigation, right?"

My legs still felt like noodles, and every time I closed my eyes, all I could see was Holly's blue face. I was ready to pack and leave as quickly as possible. "Definitely."

She sighed and pushed to her feet. "Good. Do you feel up to going with me to see if we can help Marta? I suppose the police will be here soon."

I stood, and we wove our way around the corridor to Holly's dressing room. When we rounded the last corner, we stopped. A shiny yellow crime scene ribbon stretched across the hallway. Several armed policemen milled around. Two were in deep conversation with the security guards I'd told about Holly's death. The tall blond guard looked up at us and pointed. "There she is. She's the one."

"Remind me to send John a basket of fruit or something when we get home," I muttered as I trudged into our suite two hours later.

Carly looked up then glanced over to where Zac, the twins, and Danielle were engrossed in a TV DVD game. "Marta's John?"

I shook my head. "The Lake View chief of police John."

"Why?"

"He may be a pain, but at least he never suspected me of murder." I sank down beside her on the couch and kicked off my shoes. "Those officers must have made me repeat my story twenty-five times. They were obviously hoping I'd get it wrong one time — then they'd have their murderer, before the detectives even arrived."

The phone rang and I stretched out to snag it off the end table.

"Miss Stafford?"

I frowned at the deep voice. For some reason it sounded vaguely familiar. "Yes?"

"Chief Detective Jamison here. We need you and your sister, Carly Reece, to come downstairs."

"You're kidding." I slipped my feet back in my shoes even as I said the words. "Why?"

"We have some questions for you."

"You do know I've just told about finding the body several times, right?"

"We'll expect you in the breakfast area shortly."

"Fine," I muttered.

"Miss Stafford, all exterior exits and entrances are sealed with a police guard."

"Do you think we're going to bolt?"

"Why would you say that?"

"You were warning me."

"Warning you? I just wanted you to know that it's safe to walk down here."

"We'll be right there."

Carly looked at me with a bemused expression on her face. "It didn't take long for you to develop an antagonistic relationship with the local police. How do you do that?"

"You heard, huh?"

She nodded. "Let me get my shoes on."

When we got down to the breakfast area,

there were police everywhere. Carly motioned to the small dining area where the booths gave the illusion of privacy. "Apparently they're questioning everyone in the hotel. There's Buck."

I glanced over at Holly's wayward husband who sat across from two policemen. He'd lost a lot of his swagger. "Wonder what they told the crowd?" I glanced toward the auditorium. "Surely Reagan's not still singing?"

Carly nodded to a corner where two detectives were sitting with the young woman. "She looks like she's singing, but I'm not sure what the tune is."

I couldn't hear what Reagan was saying either, but she gestured wildly. One of the men said something, and she tucked a strand of hair behind her ear and cast a nervous glance toward the opposite corner where Buck pushed to his feet. He said something loudly, but all I caught was the word "lawyer." The police nodded and escorted him away. To where, I wondered. Jail? His suite? His lawyer would surely have to come from Nashville. So at least he was buying himself some time.

"Miss Stafford, Mrs. Reece?"

We spun around.

A tall dark-haired man stepped toward us

and I gasped. "You."

Carly looked at me like I'd lost my mind. "Hawk Man," I whispered. "From the pool."

She nodded and stepped forward to extend a gracious hand. "Carly Reece."

He glanced over her shoulder at me, no recognition showing in those piercing eyes. "You must be Jenna Stafford. I'm Detective Jamison."

He motioned to a uniformed woman near the coffeepot and nodded to Carly. "Mrs. Reece, Detective Mayfield is going to ask you some questions. Miss Stafford, if you'll come with me . . ."

Carly left with the woman, and Detective Jamison looked at me.

"Small world, huh?" I quipped.

Without speaking, he led me to a small closet.

"You're kidding. You're going to interrogate me in a closet?"

"Desperate times," he said and waved a hand at one of the chairs that had obviously just been put there.

I sat. And went over the whole story again of how I found Holly. I must have gotten every detail consistent with my previous recital of events, because he didn't ask me any questions about it. He just nodded then looked up at me. "Do you know anyone who disliked Holly Wood?"

I snorted then tried desperately to make a cough out of it.

"You find that question amusing?" he asked, those truth-seeking eyes honed in on mine.

For some reason, when I'm confronted with people who won't show emotion, I want to force them to. I don't know why I'm that way, but I am. "I'm not sure I'd call it amusing, but if you'd known Holly, you'd know a better question might be, 'Who liked her?' "

"You mean besides her thousands of fans?"

I grimaced. "Well, yes, there are the fans. But in real life, most people clashed with Holly. The question was just to what degree."

"So you had a problem with Ms. Wood?"

See? Why couldn't I have just let well enough alone? "No, not really. I didn't know her well enough to have a problem with her."

"But you did notice other people 'clashing' with her. What did you know of her relationship with Reagan Curtis?"

I took a deep breath. "I'm sure Reagan didn't kill Holly. She was performing on the stage." I squashed down the memory of a robe-clad Reagan telling Buck good-bye the other morning. The last thing I wanted to do was incriminate someone falsely.

Detective Jamison stared down his hawk nose at me. And waited.

The silence stretched until I finally had to say something. No doubt just what he had in mind. "Holly and Reagan had a lot of jealousy issues. Professionally."

He made a note on his pad and looked back up at me. "Just professionally? What about personally?"

Another deep breath. Buck creeped me out and Reagan's self-centered personality irritated me, but did that mean they were murderers? "They had some personal issues, too, I imagine." I quickly told him about my first meeting with Buck and his subsequent rendezvous with Reagan.

He made a few notes while I squirmed in my chair.

"What about Holly's relationship with her sister?"

"Ruth?"

"Do you know of another sister?"

"No." For a split second, I considered offering him Carly's tattered copy of Holly's autobiography. "Ruth tried to do whatever Holly wanted. At times that was harder than others."

"Did you ever hear them argue?"

Poor Ruth. No way on earth she'd killed Holly, but I couldn't lie. I nodded.

When I finished telling him about the silly argument about the dress, he sat back in his chair. "Besides the band members, do you know anyone in the hotel who plays guitar?"

"Guitar?" Suddenly I remembered the slender plastic thread at Holly's throat. Of course. "A guitar string," I whispered.

The detective's normally implacable face flashed a hint of dismay. He obviously hadn't realized I didn't recognize the murder weapon.

"Please answer the question."

"No, I don't know anyone else who plays the guitar."

His gaze was stony now. "Do you have any idea who might have killed Ms. Wood?"

I shook my head. "No clue."

He handed me his card. "We'll need you and your sister to stay in town for a few days. I trust that won't be a problem."

"I guess not."

"Call me if you think of anything else."

When everyone was settled into bed and the kids had finally quit talking about the murder and fallen asleep, I tiptoed into Carly's room. The bathroom light gave enough illumination for me to see she was in her bed, with the navy comforter pulled up under her chin.

"I'm awake," she said. "That was pretty weird, Hawk Man and Detective Jamison being the same man, wasn't it?"

"Weird doesn't even begin to cover it. But I should have known he was a cop. He's a natural."

She raised up on one elbow. "Are you attracted to him?"

"Not really. But his ability to get immediately to the truth fascinates me."

She chuckled. "I can see why you'd envy that."

"Is this another dig at my curiosity?"

"Me? No way. You can be as curious as you want as long as we don't get drawn into this murder investigation."

"I'm pretty sure Detective Jamison can handle it without our help."

"Good. Did you get in touch with Alex?"

"No. I left a voice mail." He'd heard the news, because he called during the police interrogation and left me a message to call him. I'd wrongly assumed he'd be waiting by the phone when I finished. "Did you talk to Elliott?" The local golf pro had given Zac golf lessons, but I think Carly had been the one who'd ended up learning that she was ready to give love a second chance. They were taking it slow, but there was definitely something there.

"Yeah, he called right after I hung up with Mama and Daddy. He offered to come."

"Did you say yes?"

"I told him to wait until tomorrow and let's see what happens. If they find the murderer overnight, we may be on our way home."

"True." But it would have been nice if Alex had called and offered. Our relationship, though not exactly new, was complicated. Except for a decade of not talking, we'd been close since we were very young. It had been easy to slip back into sharing everything important with him. And I thought vice versa. Apparently with me out of town, I'd dropped down on his list of priorities.

Carly rolled over, facing me, and punched her pillow.

"Trouble sleeping?"

"Yeah, I was thinking about poor Ruth."

In the semidarkness, I squinted to see my sister's face. "The truth is, she might be better off without Holly around."

"Except that I heard someone say that Holly left a large trust fund in her will for Ruth."

"Really?" I was amazed. Had there been a tiny bit of sisterly love lurking beneath Holly's heart of stone?

"But with the stipulation that every penny be used to set up and operate a large Holly Wood Museum. With Ruth as the permanent curator."

I sighed. So much for sisterly affection. "In other words, even in death, she made sure Ruth remained her faithful servant. Sneaky."

Carly groaned. "That's exactly what I thought. Speaking of sneaky, I have a confession."

"Should I call Detective Jamison?"

"Very funny. The way I knew about the museum is I heard part of Ruth's police interrogation."

My natural curiosity pushed the question out of me, even though I hated to ask. "What else did you hear?"

Carly pushed the thick down comforter back and sat up in the bed, resting against the walnut headboard. "Something about a man, but I didn't hear enough to understand. I just caught bits and pieces. The detective who was questioning me got called away, and while she was gone, I could hear Ruth."

"Sounds like they thought she might have

a motive to kill Holly."

Carly nodded. "I know, but Ruth was so humble. And when she told the policewoman that she'd always love Holly no matter what she'd done, I felt myself tear up." She reached over and snagged the extra pillow then pressed it to her abdomen. "I really don't see why they have to dredge this all up. Some bum off the street probably wandered in and killed her."

"You think?"

"Do any of the people here seem capable of murder to you?"

I shook my head. "Not really. But we surely learned our lesson about that with Hank's murder." I shrugged and patted her foot through the comforter. "Still, it might have been a stranger."

I decided to wait until tomorrow to tell her I feared it was an inside job. But I'd been thinking about it the whole time we were getting the kids settled in. The back entrance could only be accessed with a key, unless opened from the inside. Holly wasn't likely to open the door at random, and, even though it was almost directly across the hall from her dressing room, I didn't think she could have heard someone knocking on it. So either she or someone else from inside the hotel let a stranger — a murderer — in, or the killer was already inside.

It seemed a little far-fetched that a stranger would make a trip to the Paradise, knock on the door at the exact time Holly would be in the room alone, she would let him, or — chilling thought — her in, and then the mysterious visitor would strangle her. Ergo, the killer must be someone we knew. Someone who was already in the hotel.

"You don't think it was a stranger, do you?"

I jerked a little, startled out of my reverie by her words. "It could have been." I stood and sighed. So much for not sharing my bad feeling until morning. "But I don't think so."

"We'd better get some sleep. We've got church in the morning."

"Yeah. Don't forget to say your prayers."

Even in the dim light, I could see her smile. How many times had we said that to each other right before bedtime growing up? Something about the familiar words gave me comfort, as well.

I was almost out the door when her voice stopped me. "Jenna?"

I turned back. "Yeah?"

"Did you . . . um, did you tell the detective about Marta arguing with Holly?"

My stomach lurched. "Actually I'd forgotten all about it. Did you?"

"No. But she never asked me directly." The anxiety in my sister's voice spoke volumes. Her uncharacteristic quietness since the murder interrogation hadn't been so much from all of the chaos. It had been from a guilty conscience.

"I'm sure Marta told them."

"Yeah. Surely. I wish I knew what it was about."

I started to slip out of the room but then hesitated. When Carly was in junior high, she went through a period of bad dreams. She'd come in my room right before bedtime and say, "You know, squirt . . . if you want to crash in my room tonight, you can." I'd gather up my pillow and blanket and run into her room, while she followed at a cooler pace, like she'd done me a big favor.

I cleared my throat and stepped completely back into the room. "Carly? Why don't I crash in here with you tonight?"

"Sure." She tossed the pillow back over to the other side and slid down into the bed. "If you want to."

Big sisters. They never change.

# 5

Better a little with the fear of the LORD
than great wealth with turmoil.
                                    PROVERBS 15:16

"Look at this! We're on TV."

I hopped into the main room, one sandal on and one in my hand. "Where?"

Carly motioned to the flat screen on the dresser. "Okay, not us, but the Paradise Hotel. Marta called and told me. She and John just finished making a statement to the press. They'll pick us up at the back entrance in twenty minutes for church."

On the screen, a well-known national news anchorwoman glanced at a small picture of the Paradise over her left shoulder. "As most people know by now, popular country singer, Holly Wood, was apparently murdered at this Branson, Missouri, theater last night. Now, reporting live from the Paradise is our own Colby Bell. Colby, tell us about the crowd behind you, but first, are there any new developments in this tragic event?"

I sank onto the couch and fiddled with the buckle on my sandal. "Wow. Look at all those people."

The camera zoomed in on the young man's appropriately solemn expression. "Thank you, Bridgett. We have an unsubstantiated report that Holly Wood's widower, Buck Fisher, arrived at the police station early this morning with his lawyer. It doesn't appear that any charges have been filed at this time, but we are here in Branson to keep you apprised of all the latest developments in this breaking story."

"I guess whatever time Buck bought himself last night is up now," Carly said.

I narrowed my eyes. "If he did it, why would he have come from the opposite direction when I went to Holly's dressing room last night?"

"Who knows?"

We turned our attention back to the TV. Colby Bell had moved closer to the crowd. "As you can see, an impromptu memorial has been started here in front of the Paradise. Fans have gathered here, many who have been here since last night, to pay their last respects to the beloved star." The camera panned the crowd of mourners around the candlelit teddy bear memorial.

I shook my head. "It's sad that on Sunday morning they're all here paying homage to Holly."

Carly looked up from the mirror, where she was applying a light touch of lip gloss. "Do you really think they've been here all night?"

For a split second, the camera zoomed in on one woman's anguished face. Her hair askew, her T-shirt rumpled, she stared at the candles.

I shuddered. "She definitely looks like she has." Even though Holly was dead, passion still burned in the woman's eyes. "It's kind of creepy, isn't it?"

"That she was right? That to many people, she was their life?"

The news cut to a commercial, and I hit the MUTE button. "Yeah. What would it be like to inspire that kind of devotion in just one person, much less thousands?"

"He'll call," Carly said dryly.

I laughed. "You know me too well."

My cell phone rang just as I finished speaking.

"Told you," she muttered.

I snagged it from my purse and glanced at the caller ID. Alex had finally managed to fit me into his busy schedule. "Hello?"

"Jenna? Are you okay?" His voice sounded warm but tinged with exhaustion. My irritation faded away. He truly was working hard to get his practice off the ground.

"I'm fine. You sound tired."

"Just worried about you."

*Then why didn't you call sooner?* "We're okay. We're going to leave for church in a few minutes, but I can call you back after. If you're going to be around."

A knock on the door echoed through the room. "Hang on, Alex."

"I'll get it." Carly hurried toward the door. "It's probably Marta and John."

"Don't forget to look in the peephole," I whispered.

Carly nodded.

"Good to see you're being cautious," Alex said.

Carly put her eye to the tiny hole then gasped.

"What is it?"

She shook her head as if speechless and yanked open the door.

I hurried toward her. "Alex, I'm going to have to go." Clearly, from Carly's reaction, it wasn't John and Marta, but who else would she let in?

"Okay, I wouldn't want to keep you from

79

your company," his deep voice boomed through the room.

I glanced at the phone, wondering for a brief second if I'd accidentally hit the SPEAKER button.

"Hey, water girl. You fall into the deep end without even trying, don't you?"

I looked up into his gorgeous blue eyes and smiled, sympathizing with Carly's speechlessness.

Carly cleared her throat. "I'm going to go check and see if the kids are ready for church." She hurried out of the room.

Alex closed the door behind him and stepped toward me. "When I couldn't get in touch with you, I threw some things in the truck and drove up here. I hope that was okay."

"More than okay."

He folded me into his arms. "I was worried about you," he whispered against my hair.

Tears sprang to my eyes as I listened to his steady heartbeat. "Thank you for coming."

"Nothing could have kept me away. It was so late when I got in town last night, I was afraid you were asleep. And I couldn't get within a mile of the Paradise. So I booked a room at a hotel down the road. This morning I decided to surprise you with an escort to church."

I pushed back and looked at him, still having a hard time believing he was really here. "How did you get past security?"

"I got here right after Marta's press conference. I introduced myself, showed her some ID, and she let me in." He motioned toward the TV. "That's even scarier live. I was thankful she was there."

The fans were still singing and swaying, holding candles and roses. The woman I'd noticed earlier was still in the front row. I stepped over to the couch, snagged the remote, and hit the POWER button.

Hayley and Rachel came barreling into the room. "Hi, Alex," they chorused.

Zac ambled in behind them. "Hey, man." He and Alex touched knuckles in greeting.

"Marta called again. They're waiting at the back." Carly grabbed her Bible and purse from the desk and grinned at me. "She seemed to think you had another ride."

She waggled her fingers and shepherded the kids out. "See you there," she called over her shoulder.

I glanced up at Alex.

He raised an eyebrow. "That's assuming you trust me to drive you?"

"If I remember correctly, you did assure

me that your NASCAR-wannabe days are behind you. So I guess I'm safe."

As he rested an easy hand on the small of my back and escorted me into the hall, I admitted something to myself. I not only felt safe with Alex, I felt like I was exactly where I belonged.

I opened my mouth to try to tell him what I was thinking, but just then I saw a figure step away from the doorway of Buck and Holly's suite and start in the opposite direction.

"Hey!" I called instinctively. The man glanced back for a split second, but it was enough time for me to recognize him as Holly's guitar player, Joey. I started toward him, but he broke into a sprint and soon was out of sight.

A hand on my arm made me turn around. "Jenna? Is something wrong?"

I nodded. "I think he just came out of Buck and Holly's suite."

Alex raised an eyebrow. "Is he a stranger?"

I shook my head. "He's in the band."

"So he was probably paying his respects to the widower."

"Except that Buck is at the police station with his lawyer."

He sighed. "Jenna, I'm sure he had a legitimate reason for being in the room.

Besides, we didn't even see him come out the door for sure; he could have just dropped something and picked it up."

Men and their logic. "I guess, but why did he run?"

"Because you sounded like you thought he was a criminal."

"What if he is?"

Alex frowned. "You're going to try to solve this murder, aren't you?"

"Not necessarily."

He looked harder, worry lines deepening between his eyes.

"I can't just ignore something like this, can I?"

For a second he didn't speak; then his words came slowly. "I'd like to think you could. You definitely should." He blew out a pent-up breath. "But I know you won't."

"Does that bother you?"

He stopped and faced me. "It hasn't been that long since your curiosity almost got you killed. Do you honestly think I could not be worried about you getting involved?" He pushed my hair back from my face and looked directly into my eyes. "I —"

My heart slammed against my ribs. He was finally going to say it.

"You're very important to me."

■ ■ ■ ■

After church, the kids talked us into going to the Uptown Café. The twins, along with Zac and Danielle, commandeered the soda counter. The rest of us crowded into a retro booth, with me sandwiched between Carly and Alex.

As soon as we ordered, Alex looked at John and Marta. "You two okay?"

John nodded. "We're going to be fine. As sad as Holly's death is, the Paradise will make it through."

Marta's eyebrows knitted together. "You're being overly optimistic, honey."

"We can reopen by the first of next month if the police will hurry and clear this up." John sounded bone tired but determined.

"Yeah? And who will want to perform where the star got killed? Especially with the murderer still on the loose." I could tell Marta had repeated this sentence or a variation of it several times. This was obviously an ongoing discussion. "We might as well admit it, John, this is the end of our dreams. I should start looking for a job."

My eyes widened. In all the years I had known her, Marta had never given up on anything she set her mind to. She'd bounce back from this. "You can't quit."

Carly leaned forward and covered Marta's hand with hers. "Maybe we can help you find the murderer, at least."

Alex stiffened beside me. I elbowed Carly. What had happened to us staying out of this investigation?

Marta gave Carly a teary smile. "We'd better just let the police do their job, but thanks."

"Wonder where the funeral will be?" I asked, hoping the subject change was subtle enough not to be obvious.

Carly jumped in to help. "Nashville, I'm sure. With a huge monument and eternal flame."

"That would be one way of guaranteeing our place's success," John said dryly. "We could offer to build a mausoleum in front of the Paradise."

Marta gasped. "John!"

He put his arm around her. "I'm just kidding. I promise."

The waitress brought our burgers and passed them out. She clutched the tray to her chest. "Did you folks hear about Holly Wood?"

We nodded.

Tears sprang to her already red-rimmed eyes. "It's sad that's what people will always remember Branson for."

Now it was Marta's turn to cry. John tightened his arm around her. "Murder can happen anywhere."

The waitress shrugged, obviously not picking up on his gruff voice. "I guess."

She left and Marta turned her face into John's shoulder.

"Marta," Carly said softly. "Holly's death wasn't your fault."

"I'm so selfish," Marta said, her voice muffled. "I only thought about it ruining our business. I didn't even think about us taking Branson's reputation down with us."

John motioned to the full restaurant. "It doesn't look like we've single-handedly destroyed Branson's good name yet. Think about that pile of teddy bears and flowers out in front of the theater. It sounds callous, but the truth is, tourist trade may go up. People will come here just to be near where Holly died." He squirted ketchup on Marta's plate and even dipped the first french fry for her.

She obediently took the fry and popped it into her mouth. "It all depends on the murderer being caught quickly."

"You know, John," Alex said quietly, "Your idea of a memorial for Holly at the Paradise isn't all that crazy."

I jerked around to look at him. I knew he was desperate to get us off the subject of finding the murderer. But was he seriously suggesting that John and Marta build a mausoleum at their theater?

"What about hosting a memorial concert? In a couple of weeks. After the funeral."

Carly clapped her hands together softly. "That's a wonderful idea!"

Marta fiddled with her cheeseburger. "Don't you think people would think that we were capitalizing on tragedy?"

I shrugged. "We can't control what people think, but if I were a fan, I'd love a memorial concert. Let's face it. There won't be room for the world at Holly's funeral. This would give people closure."

John wiped his mouth. "She's right, honey. Plus we could recoup a little of our loss from last night's concert."

She drew back and stared at him in horror. "We are *not* charging people to come to Holly's memorial concert."

"But expenses . . ." John's voice faded away.

"God will take care of the details," Marta said.

See? I knew it wouldn't take long for the old Marta to return.

"And we're not about to profit from her

death," she finished.

"Fat chance of that," John mumbled, but he reached over and took his wife's hand. "We'll give them a few days then talk to Buck and Ruth about it."

"Assuming the police don't arrest Buck," I murmured.

Marta ignored me and grabbed an ink pen and a napkin. "Buck, Ruth . . ." She scrawled names as she talked. "What about Maurice Seaton? I wonder if he'll come to Branson?"

At Alex's confused expression, I whispered, "Holly's first husband and her long-time financial advisor. Oh, and he's from Lake View."

Marta continued, "He loved Holly so much. I bet he'll be grief stricken, but he could help us." She added his name to her list.

She looked so much more hopeful that I resisted the urge to remind her that she was going to let God take care of the details.

"Didn't Holly say she had a personal assistant?" Carly offered. "Maybe she could help."

Marta shook her head. "Cindy Cunningham. I called her last night. Turns out Holly didn't give her time off. She fired her."

"Why would Holly lie about it?" I couldn't

see the logic. "Did Cindy say why she got fired?"

"No. But she didn't seem terribly upset about Holly's death."

Carly pursed her lips. "Was she surprised?"

"She didn't say and I couldn't decide. I think she'd probably already heard it on the news."

"Did you call her home phone?" I asked quietly.

Marta frowned. "No, it was her cell."

"So she could have been anywhere."

Carly grabbed my arm. "Like in town getting revenge."

Alex cleared his throat. "Y'all don't have any trouble jumping to conclusions, do you?"

I grinned at him. "We're athletically inclined like that. But the good news is, we do rein it in sooner or later."

"More sooner than later, I hope."

The twins came running over to us. "Zac and Danielle said they'd take us to ride the go-karts!"

Marta and Carly exchanged a look, and I could read it as clearly as if they'd spoken aloud. Not with a murderer loose in town.

"What if we all go?" I asked them quietly.

They both nodded. The kids bounded off

to tell the teens, and John and Marta stood.

"If it's okay with you," I added to Alex.

He grinned at me. "Looks like I'd better hang around close to keep you from getting in over your head."

"Don't worry. I know how to swim."

"Everybody gets a cramp now and then and needs a buddy."

Carly rolled her eyes. "Would you guys just say what you mean?"

I laughed. "Did you forget he's a lawyer?"

Alex put his hand to his heart. "Are you implying I don't say what I mean?"

"If the Italian leather loafer fits . . ." I threw over my shoulder then hurried out before he could cross-examine me.

# 6

Anger is cruel and fury
overwhelming, but who can
stand before jealousy?
PROVERBS 27:4

Alex and I watched the kids ride for a while, but then I noticed in between laps, he'd close his eyes. "You must be worn out," I said softly during one of those times.

His eyes flew open, and he looked over at me. "I'm sorry I wasn't here."

"You had to work. I understand that." In spite of my momentary diva lapse when he called Friday and cancelled, I was adult enough to get the concept of needing to work. Of course, I was also adult enough to know some people use work for an excuse to avoid personal commitment.

"I should have been with you when you found the body." He reached over and knitted his fingers through mine.

"Alex, you can't protect me from everything."

"I can try," he said, the quiet words almost lost in the roar of the go-karts passing by.

"You drove half the night. If you're going to be Superman to my Lois Lane, you'd better get a nap first. I'm ready to go if you are."

He smiled. "I do feel like I've been a little too close to kryptonite. What if I go back and rest for just a bit, then take you to a show tonight?"

I gave him my best cheesy grin. "Sounds super."

We said our good-byes to John, Marta, and Carly then walked out to the parking lot.

Alex opened my door and gave me a hand up into the four-wheel-drive truck.

On the road to the hotel, I grabbed my cell phone. "I meant to ask Marta about getting you in a room."

He shook his head. "Marta's got enough on her mind. As much as I'd like to be closer to you, I'm already settled in where I stayed last night."

"You sure that's okay?"

He nodded and pulled into the Paradise entrance. I stared at the huge mound of teddy bears, flowers, candles, and letters.

Alex let out a low whistle. "Will you look at that!" Even more fans were crowded together in the hot sun. Police officers milled around the crowd, and while we watched, a young blond collapsed onto the concrete. A female cop bent down to her, talking on her radio at the same time.

"Talk about pandemonium."

"I'll walk you in," Alex said.

"If you don't mind just driving me around to the back, I think I can slip in by myself. I didn't get much sleep last night either. I might try to catch a nap, too."

When we got to the back entrance, there was no one in sight. Alex got out and held the truck door open for me. He pulled me toward him and dropped a light kiss on the top of my head. "Stay out of trouble."

I laughed. "Always."

He raised an eyebrow. "I wish. Call me after your nap."

"What if you're still asleep?"

He brushed my hair back from my face. "Some things are more important than sleep. Call me."

I slid my key into the slot, pulled open the door, and stepped into the cool hallway. What kind of loyalty would persuade people to stand for hours out in the hot June afternoon sun? As I passed Holly's dressing room, I noticed the yellow police tape sagging low in front of the door. I looked both ways and carefully turned the knob. It opened easily.

A little frisson of nauseous déjà vu skittered in my stomach as I looked at her chair. But there was nothing to indicate that a dead body once sat there. As I stepped over the tape and into the room, the sliding closet door, slightly ajar, caught my eye. Detective Jamison's men weren't as tidy as they should have been. I walked over to close it and glanced in at the shimmering materials and jewel-bright colors of Holly's wardrobe. Poor Holly. She'd always dressed so vibrantly. It was still hard to believe she was dead.

I shut the closet door firmly. I needed to get out of here. Some places aren't meant to be snooped in. I was almost to the door when a soft, swishing sound came from the closet. My first impulse was to dash from the room and padlock the door. But curiosity moved my feet toward the noise. Just before I touched the handle, the door slid open with a *bang.* A body erupted from the closet, pushing me backward by pure momentum.

"Don't you ever close a door on me again," the blur of motion said. "I can't stand to be in a small space." Reagan caught her balance and advanced on me.

I took another step backward. "I'm sorry," I said instinctively in the face of her fury.

"What are you doing in here anyway?" She glared at me. "Going through Holly's stuff? Maybe trying to find something to sell on eBay? Some people have no shame." She moved to go around me as I took in the insults she spewed at me. I came to my senses in time to block the door.

"More to the point, what were *you* doing in Holly's closet?" I gave her the look Carly gives the twins when they're trying to pull one over on her. But Reagan was made of sterner stuff. Instead of wilting and confessing all, she pushed me out of the way and grasped the doorknob. I closed my hand over her hand on the knob and held it still. We were both huffing and puffing like two kids fighting over the same toy. Reagan must be guilty of something or she wouldn't have gone on the defensive so quickly.

"Reagan," I panted. I paused for a deep breath and voice control. "Reagan," I tried again, and thankfully, it came out sounding a bit more mature. "Why *were* you in Holly's closet? If you don't want me to call Detective Jamison immediately, you have to tell me." I shot her a nervous look. I could hear Alex's voice in my head. I don't think this is what he meant by staying out of trouble. Had I just threatened a murderer? I tightened my grasp on her hand.

She grunted. "Good grief. Don't get your panties in a wad. I was just" — she paused and her eyes darted around as if searching for inspiration — "looking for a scarf Holly borrowed from me." I followed her gaze to the coat rack and saw a blue scarf.

"Come on, Reagan. Tell me the truth." I tried to sound tough.

She bit her lip. "Actually . . ." Her hand on the doorknob relaxed. I loosened my grip in response.

She yanked open the door and dashed out.

"Well, that went well," I muttered to the empty room.

Adrenaline still pumping, I leaned against the door to catch my breath. What had Reagan been doing in the closet? I tiptoed back to the rows of glittery clothes, half afraid that a left-behind cohort would jump out at me. I wasn't sure whether to be disappointed or relieved to find nothing out of the ordinary. I chose relieved and hurried from the dressing room.

As I approached Holly and Buck's suite, the door started to open. I stopped and took a deep breath. Had Joey not finished with his business in there this morning? I stared at the doorway and waited.

I blew out my breath as Buck Fisher stepped out of his room, a suitcase in his hand and a hanging garment bag across his arm. His eyes were red-rimmed, and overnight his face seemed to have aged. Either he was truly sad or a fantastic actor.

I nodded and started to move on by.

He touched my arm with his free hand. "Jenna, right?"

"Yes."

He reached in his pocket and pulled out a turquoise money clip bulging with green. He peeled a hundred dollar bill from the stack. "Would you have someone pack up Holly's things and send them to our Nashville address?"

He pressed the money and a business card into my hand, along with a room key.

"I'll be glad to do it. You don't have to —"

He shook his head. "It's worth it to me not to have to handle them right now."

His voice rang with sincerity, and I was overwhelmed with a crazy sympathy for this man who had undoubtedly cheated on the Queen of Country Music. "I understand." I took the card and the key, but I shoved the money back to him.

"Please keep it," he said.

I shook my head. "No, but thank you. I'll let you reimburse me for shipping. Where are you going?" Okay, I knew I was pushing it, but I hoped he'd answer anyway.

He sighed as he added the bill back to his stash. "The cops gave me permission to go to Nashville and take care of business there. Make funeral arrangements."

"Oh, don't forget to let someone in Lake View know what date you pick." Lame, but totally normal for me in these kinds of situations.

He gave me a blank look.

"Holly's from my hometown. And we're all so sorry for your loss."

"Oh, thank you. I'm sure the funeral arrangements will be well reported." His smile was a shadow of his former cheesy grin. "So Lake View will know along with the rest of the world."

My cheeks grew hot. He'd certainly put me in my place.

I went back to our suite to wait for Alex to wake up from his nap, all the while feeling a little like Alice in Wonderland. Maybe I'd fallen asleep and dreamed of Reagan in Holly's dressing room closet and Buck giving me carte blanche to their suite. I lay back on the bed and ran my thumb over

Buck's business card. Holly's body hadn't been a figment of my imagination and neither was the fact that there was a murderer among us.

This was the real deal. And my pounding heart every time I thought about crossing that police tape proved that Alex was right.

I was in over my head.

"I haven't laughed that much in so long," I said, as we exited the comedy theater. "Thanks for taking me."

Alex hooked his arm through mine and leaned in close to my ear. "You have a beautiful laugh. I've missed hearing it."

I shivered. "I've only been gone for a few days."

"Seems like longer."

"It does, doesn't it?" Even finding Holly's body last night seemed so far away. So much had happened.

When the double doors opened, the blast of hot air hit me. At ten o'clock at night, the air was still sticky hot. Alex held my hand as we walked out to his truck. He hit the UNLOCK button on the key fob then opened the door for me. His parents had raised him right. He's a throwback to a more gentlemanly generation, and I loved it.

When he slid into his own seat, he started the motor and turned the air on but didn't put the motor in gear. "You know, Jenna, unless you really need me to stay, I have to be in court Tuesday morning."

I swallowed against a sudden lump in my throat. It wasn't like I'd thought he could stay forever. But I wasn't ready to say good-bye. Even for a short while. I nodded, not trusting myself to speak.

"So I guess I'll head home tomorrow after-noon."

So soon? *Keep it light,* I coached myself. "Well, Counselor Campbell, as much as I'd like for you to stay, I know your clients are counting on you to play Superman for them. Will we be able to do something together in the morning before you put on the cape?"

A boyish grin flashed across his face. "I was hoping we would. If I won't be hinder-ing your investigation."

I stared up at him. I hadn't wanted to keep my "investigation" secret from him, but I hadn't trusted him not to overreact. Was he giving me tacit permission to look into the murder? "Any 'investigating' can wait until Tuesday," I said, part seriously and part tongue-in-cheek.

"Want to tell me what you've found so far?"

I tried to read his eyes.

He laughed. "Even in the moonlight, I recognize that you-can't-handle-the-truth look. Lay it on me, Stafford. I'm tougher than you think."

"More powerful than a locomotive. I know, I've heard." I made a split-second decision. It was time for me to commit. Not by saying "I love you" first, because there was nothing wrong with me waiting to hear it from him, but I needed to commit by trusting him. Trusting him to keep my secrets and respect my decisions. "Well, you know what happened in the hall with Joey, the guitar player, this morning. Which may or may not be anything."

"Right. And?"

I quickly told him about finding Reagan in the closet.

"You crossed the police tape?" His voice didn't squeak, but it definitely rose in tone.

I should have stopped while I was ahead. I nodded without speaking.

He took a deep breath. "That took a lot of nerve."

"Thanks."

"And was completely illegal."

Now it was his turn to learn to stop while

he was ahead.

"Well, it was sagging and looked almost like they'd just forgotten they put it there. You could tell lots of people have been in and out of there." I cringed. "Okay, I admit it. I shouldn't have gone in. I didn't stop and think before I stepped over that tape. I've felt awful ever since. Does that count for anything?"

He reached over and touched my shoulder. "Don't beat yourself up. Your natural curiosity is one of the things that makes you so special." He pulled slowly out onto the highway. "So why do you think Reagan was in there?"

"I have no idea. She and Buck were . . . kind of close . . . before Holly died." I gave him a quick rundown on the morning I found them with Reagan in her robe. "But it also seemed like Holly was Reagan's standard — the one singer she compared herself to. She could have gone in her dressing room to get closure."

Alex frowned. "Or tamper with evidence."

"True. But we left Holly's room the first time at seven sharp. Exactly the time Reagan took the stage. And during the break when Holly was supposed to come out, Reagan was only gone five . . . maybe ten minutes."

"Long enough to commit murder," he said flatly as we pulled into the hotel entrance.

I motioned to the candle-holding group still lingering around the makeshift memorial. "Then come back out and sing to a packed crowd?" That seemed cold — but then, I guess if she were a killer . . .

He shrugged as he drove around back. "The show must go on." Instead of pulling over to the hotel's door, he backed the truck into a parking place and let the engine idle. He turned slightly in his seat to face me and locked his gaze with mine. "Make no mistake, Jenna. This isn't a game. You are dealing with a killer who is capable of anything. Including killing again."

"I know. I'm being careful."

He sighed. "I hope so. I'd hate to lose you."

"I'd hate that, too." I half laughed, a feeble attempt to lighten the mood.

He smiled. "So we're on for tomorrow?"

"Definitely. What do you have planned?"

"Oh, I think I'll just keep our itinerary a mystery. That way I know you'll show up."

"You're a very funny guy. Tell me."

"Here's a clue. Dress outdoor casual. And be at the back entrance at seven."

"Are you serious? You're not going to tell me what we're doing?"

He leaned toward me and brushed my hair back.

"Is this a plan to distract me from my questions?" I whispered.

"Maybe," he whispered back, his face close to mine.

"It's working."

"Good." He dropped a light kiss on my lips, but before I could respond, he put the engine in gear and pulled up to the hotel back entrance.

Without a word, he jumped out and came around to hold my door open.

He walked with me to the door and waited while I slid my key. But as soon as I stepped inside, I glanced back, and he was standing by his truck, watching me.

So much for long good-byes.

# 7

A hot-tempered man stirs up dissension,
but a patient man calms a quarrel.
PROVERBS 15:18

"You have no idea where you're going?" Carly squinted against the morning sun and sat on the edge of her bed, blanket nubbies marking the side of her face. She sleepily watched me put on my socks and tennis shoes.

I shook my head and pulled my shoe up to tie it. "None. Just 'outdoor casual,' whatever that means. What are you doing today?"

"I think the kids and I will just hang out within walking distance. Dani will probably spend the day with us."

"Keep an eye out for Reagan, Car."

She cocked her head at me. "Why?"

I quickly told her about my closet encounter. "And Joey, too."

"Holly's guitar player is on your suspect list?"

I nodded and tied my other shoe. "I think I saw him coming out of Holly and Buck's suite yesterday morning while Buck was at the police station."

"So thanks to the news report, he would have known that Buck was gone."

"Exactly. And we know the murder weapon was a guitar string. Which could actually incriminate either of them."

"That settles it. We'll steer clear of Reagan and Joey, I promise. You forget all this and enjoy Alex's last day in town."

Something in her voice made me do a double take. Why did I have a feeling she was thinking about her golf pro and wishing she was enjoying Branson with him? "Are you sorry you told Elliott not to come?"

She shrugged. "Sure. A little. But I'm not ready for that kind of commitment."

As I walked down to the back entrance to meet Alex, I thought about Carly's words. I wondered if Alex would have still come if he'd realized his Branson trip constituted commitment?

We rode in silence for a while; then Alex whipped the truck into a parking lot and killed the motor.

I nodded toward the big white letters on the side of the building. "A day at Wal-Mart. I can see why you kept this such a big secret."

"Funny girl. Let's go."

"Good thing you told me to dress casual," I murmured as we got out of the truck.

He put his arm around my shoulders. "If I could have done this part without you, I would have."

I looked up at him. "That's so romantic."

He winked. "Just wait."

Inside, we said hello to the door greeter, and Alex guided me toward the back of the store.

"If you tell me where we're going, you won't have to hold on to me."

He grinned. "I don't mind."

Truthfully, neither did I. The big johnboat suspended from the ceiling and the rows of camouflage gave it away. "What are we doing in sporting goods?" I whispered.

Alex turned to the white-haired man behind the counter. "We need a couple of out-of-state fishing licenses."

"We're going fishing?" Alex and I used to fish together when we were young. Since he'd moved back to Lake View, we'd talked a lot about it but never done it.

"Shh . . ." he said out of the side of his

107

mouth. "It's a surprise for my girlfriend."

At least he knew I was his girlfriend. Unfortunately I was looking for a little more assurance for the future.

I handed the clerk my driver's license and looked over at the brightly colored lures hanging on a display. "Won't we need fishing tackle?"

Alex grinned. "I've got it all taken care of. Trust me."

Believe me, if I didn't, I wouldn't still be hanging around . . . waiting.

An hour later, all my cares had melted away with the heat of the sun reflecting off Lake Taneycomo. I could lose myself in the soft sloshing of the water. Even the distant motor sounds created a sort of white noise conducive to forgetting everything. My contention with Lisa at the health club . . . a distant memory. Even Holly's murder and all Marta's troubles took a break from the forefront of my mind. I looked over at Alex, kicked back in his boat chair, his fishing pole stuck in the holder beside him. His eyes were closed and the bill of his cap shaded his face.

"Are you letting it all go?" he asked without opening his eyes.

"Yes. Thank you." I watched the water for

ripples or other evidence of fish. "Are you?"

He reached and still without looking grabbed my hand. "I'm not thinking about letting go."

I shivered. "Good."

His eyes popped open, and his gaze met mine. "Cold?"

I shook my head. "This was the perfect idea."

He sat up slowly. He pointed toward a cluster of buildings on the far shore. "See that campground over there? I spent some great times there with my folks when I was a kid." Suddenly his rod bucked. He snatched it loose from the holder and began to reel.

I grabbed the net just as the fish broke the surface of the water, still attached to his line. Its fins sparkled like a treasure trove. "Easy to see why they call it a rainbow trout, isn't it?"

"It's a nice size. Think Carly will want to cook trout for y'all's supper?"

I nodded. "If Marta's not using her kitchen, then she definitely would."

He undid the hook and dropped the fish into the live well.

We sat down again, our lines drifting across the peaceful water.

I laid my head back. "I'd love to come out

here at night. I bet there are a million stars."

He nodded. "When dad and I used to night fish out here, we'd play amateur astronomer and try to name all the constellations." He pointed toward the shore. "The North Star comes up right over the campground."

"I'm glad you and your parents did things together. In my distorted memory, it seems like I took all of your dad's time with my swimming."

He laughed. "You worry too much about the past. I had a normal childhood. You, on the other hand . . ."

"Hey!" I slapped at him. "My childhood was normal. Except for the twenty hours a week I spent swimming."

"If you ever have kids, do you think you'll encourage them to do something so demanding?"

I squinted into the sunlight, hoping that any moisture in my eyes would be attributed to that. If *I* ever have kids? Not if *we* ever have kids, but if *I* ever have kids . . . I'd let this relationship get out of balance. I seriously needed to reevaluate what I was doing with Alex. If this is what I wanted for the rest of my life — a boyfriend — then I had it made. But if I was looking for more, then I probably needed to move on.

"I mean . . . not that there's anything wrong with your childhood. I just wondered. It seems like a lot of pressure for a kid."

I cleared my throat and fiddled with my reel. "I guess that would just be a decision my husband and I would have to make based on what's best for our child." Whoa. Did the day suddenly get colder or was it just me?

"That makes sense."

This time my pole buckled. Relieved, I stood and reeled in a good-sized trout. Alex netted it and took it off my hook, then dropped it in with the other one.

For a while we fished in silence. What was Alex thinking? Did he know I was hurt, or was he so unaware of my feelings that he didn't even realize?

Thankfully, we caught a few more fish right in a row, making conversation not impossible, but unnecessary.

Alex grinned. "You hungry?"

I'd lost my appetite back when he asked me about if *I* had a child, but I wasn't going to tell him that. "Are we going to the shore for lunch?"

"You'll see."

He started the motor and puttered due north to the campground he'd shown me earlier. When he lifted a blanket and re-

111

trieved a wicker basket from the back of the boat, my jaw dropped. "You made us a picnic lunch?"

He ducked his head and shot me a wry grin. "I ordered it from a local deli. But it's the thought that counts, right?"

"Right." I let him help me out of the boat.

He spread the blanket out on a small spot of green grass and set the basket down next to a scraggly pine. We had a perfect view of the lake.

The sub sandwiches were delicious, complete with fresh, crisp pickles and chips. Alex proudly poured me some cold lemonade.

It was hard to stay upset when he was so kind, but I had to remind myself of my earlier epiphany. Did I want a life of spontaneous fishing trips and surprise picnics? Or did I want home and hearth? Or both? "This is great, Alex. But I bet it was a lot of trouble to arrange."

"Nothing's too much trouble for you."

Aww. Now see? Every time I thought about walking away, he'd do or say something sweet like that.

Carly looked up from her chair as I walked in. "You look tired." She took a second look. "But happy. And sunburned. Didn't you wear sunblock?"

I touched my hot face. "I did actually. I forgot to reapply it, and then I fell asleep for a while."

"Oh Jenna. I'm sorry."

"I haven't pulled a stunt like that since college. But the time just flew."

She grinned. "It does that when you're having fun. Did he finally say it?"

I shrugged. "In words? No. But in every other way that counts, yes. He even let me bring you the fish we caught, cleaned and ready to cook." I lifted the tiny cooler for her to see.

Her face lit up, and she jumped to her feet. "How did you know I needed to cook? I already called Marta and told her I'd be fixing supper for all of us."

"Why? Is something wrong?"

"Not really wrong. But I found out something a little odd while you were gone." She glanced toward the sitting room where the kids were playing a rowdy game of Cranium. She lowered her voice. "I think you might be right about Joey."

"Oh?" So she *was* serious about investigating? This was a new Carly. "When did you go all Miss Marple on me?"

She looked pleased but shook her head. "This info fell into my lap, actually. At

113

lunch, we were talking about Holly's band, and Danielle said that Joey hated Holly."

I leaned toward her to catch the last words. "Why?" I mouthed.

"Seems Holly took his dad away from his mom."

"So at one point she was his stepmom?"

Carly shrugged. "I'm not sure if Joey's dad was one of the husbands or not. Dani didn't mention that."

"It really doesn't matter. His father ditching his mother for Holly gives Joey the perfect reason to hate her."

"And kill her? So should we tell Detective Jamison?" Carly asked.

"Not yet. All we have at this point is hearsay. But it's enough for me to have a talk with Joey."

"You're just going to march down to his suite?"

"Don't be silly. I'm going to meet him in the lobby. Wanna come?"

She held her hands out as if they were scales. "Let's see . . . cook. Or confront a possible killer." She took the cooler from my hand and started for the door. "If you need me, I'll be in Marta's kitchen at her cottage. Supper will be ready at 6:30."

I used the house phone in the lobby to be

connected to Joey's suite, and after the second ring, I heard a gruff, "Huh?"

Clearly I'd awakened the sleeping beauty from his afternoon nap.

"Hello," I chirped. "This is Jenna Stafford, the Hills' assistant, and I need to talk with you. Please meet me in the lobby." Hopefully that sounded professional enough that he wouldn't ask any questions.

"W–h–y should I?" He sounded like a particularly touchy bear prematurely awakened from hibernation. This should be fun. And so much for my professionalism.

"W–e–ll." I drew the word out in a drawl Carly could be proud of. "We can just skip our talk, and I can go straight to Detective Jamison with the information I've obtained. I just thought you might want to hear it first. Maybe clear things up a bit?"

"I don't know what you're talking about." The bear voice sounded slightly quivery now. Like maybe he'd accidentally put his paw in a beehive. "But I'll meet with you if I have to. Give me a few minutes."

I'd barely fixed a cup of coffee from the lobby pot when Joey appeared, wearing a black shirt with a guitar played by skeleton hands emblazoned on the front and some gray army-style pants. His stand-straight-up hair and five-o'clock shadow completed the scruffy rock star look. Since I was the only person in the large open area — so much for my great plan of safety in numbers — he walked right over to me. "You the one who called me?"

I stood. "Yes. I'm Jenna Stafford."

"Congratulations. What's this about the police?" The venomous look in his eye caused me to back up a little. Maybe this wasn't such a great idea after all.

"Why don't we sit down?" I motioned toward the two chairs that framed the table with the coffeepot.

He growled. "No."

"Er, how about a cup of coffee?" He'd obviously gotten up on the wrong side of the bed. Maybe caffeine would soothe the savage beast. I poured another cup of the steaming stuff and shuffled it across the table toward him, the angry bear analogy still fresh in my mind. He gave the cup a contemptuous look, which he then transferred to me. I decided to cut to the chase.

"I . . . I . . . heard that maybe Holly was your stepmom." I cleared my throat. That wasn't quite as emphatic as I had intended it to be. "Is that true?" At least I had quit talking about coffee and sitting and had gotten down to why we were here. That was a start.

"What business is that of yours?" He seemed to tower over me as he shoved the coffee to one side.

"Joey, you need to tell the police if there's a connection between you and Holly. If someone else tells them, you'll look guilty."

"So what are you saying? You're the one that's going to tell them?" If looks could kill . . . Holly wouldn't be the only victim.

"Well," I temporized. "Someone will. If I found out about it, obviously others already know. It would be better for you if you give them all the facts yourself. That way, they won't get any twisted story."

"Twisted? You don't know nothin' about my life." He clenched his fists and glared at me. "So what if Holly shacked up with my old man? My life is none of your business."

"No, you're right, it isn't my business. I was only trying to help."

"I don't need your help. So butt out." Before I could reply, Joey slammed both hands on the table, and the coffee cup crashed to the floor, splashing hot coffee everywhere. With a mocking smirk, he turned and strode from the room, leaving his inept questioner — aka me — to clean up his mess.

While I was still on my knees swiping up

the last of the liquid, my cell phone rang. I fished it from my pocket and flipped it open. "Hello?" I tried to sound upbeat instead of nearly beaten up.

"Jenna? This is Gail." If she hadn't said my name, I'd have thought it was a wrong number, because this woman sounded beyond agitated. The Gail I knew was a sweet-tempered college student who worked part-time at Lake View Athletic Club.

"Hey, Ga—"

"When are you coming home?"

"I —"

"If you don't hurry, there won't be anything to come home to. Lisa is ruining the club. Half the members have threatened to quit. Do you know what she's doing?"

"Well, not ex—"

"I'll tell you what she's doing."

I had a feeling she would. I clambered off the floor and onto a chair. I probably needed to be sitting for this one.

"For starters, she didn't gather towels to send to the cleaning service. Do you know how happy people were when they got out of the hot tub and pool to find they didn't have anything to dry with? And guess who they got mad at? Me."

I barely had time to grunt before she continued. "And do you know what else she did? I'll tell you." She was off again. "She didn't measure the chlorine when she serviced the pool. She just dumped it in. A lot. Amelia's new hot pink bikini turned as pastel as a baby blanket. She threatened to sue. Sue! Over a bikini. Can you believe it?"

Maybe if it was a designer bikini. Which, knowing Amelia, it probably was. "Unfortunately I can believe it."

"Well, that's not the worst. Some people burned their eyes so badly they had to have eyewash right then."

I gasped. Surely she was exaggerating.

"Only guess who took the medicine kit home with her and forgot to bring it back? But naturally, she wasn't on duty when all this happened. I was. So who do you think got chewed out? I'm telling you, Jenna, if you don't come home soon, this club will be closed. The only running Lisa's doing is running it into the ground."

She took a deep breath.

"Gail, I'm sorry, but the truth is —"

"Amelia said to tell you they're getting up a petition, and if things don't get better, they're all quitting."

Ouch. One thing I knew about the First Lady of Lake View. She didn't make idle threats. I waited a second to be sure Gail was out of steam before I attempted a reply.

"Have you talked to Bob? He's the owner, after all. He won't want the place to fall apart."

"All Bob says is that we have to give Lisa time. And that you'll be back in a few days."

That figures. Same old scenario. Bob assuming I'd feel sorry for him and cut my vacation short.

"I'm sorry to dump on you like this, Jenna, but I don't know what else to do. We'll all lose our jobs if the club closes."

I sighed quietly. As much as I had a right to be mad at Bob for how he'd treated me — promising me the health club at a good price, then bringing in Lisa instead for me to "train," or what I call "wait on hand and foot" — I couldn't let all my coworkers lose their jobs. "I'll talk to Bob."

"Thanks, Jenna. And hurry back!"

I hung up and shook my head.

"Jenna?" A trembling voice behind me made me spin around.

Holly's sister, Ruth. And a male friend. "I'd like you to meet Maurice Seaton."

I nodded. Holly's ex. Twice, actually. No wonder he looked so sad.

"Maury, Jenna Stafford. She's from Lake View, just like we are. Though she's a little younger, of course."

"Oh?" Maurice gave me a blank look from

red-rimmed eyes. "Hello."

His grief was so real that shame almost overwhelmed me. My main emotion over Holly's death, other than shock, had been dismay on behalf of John and Marta.

"I'm so sorry about your — Holly." Oops. Almost said "your wife." I don't know how long I stood there with my mouth open, trying to think of just the right word. Where was Ms. Social Graces Carly when I needed her? "Holly. About your loss." How lame. No wonder, with one foot in my mouth. "It's nice to meet you." I started to edge away, but Ruth stepped toward me and Maurice obediently followed.

"Jenna was an Olympic swimmer."

Maurice nodded, but I didn't really see any recognition on his face.

"Well, I bet you remember her older sister, Carly." Ruth seemed to be trying desperately to bring the man to life. "They saved Holly a seat on the school bus every day."

A gleam flickered in those dull eyes. "Little girl with black curly hair? I remember her. There were two of them. Twins, weren't they?"

"Just good friends." Ruth patted his shoulder as if giving him points for trying. "They're here, too — both of them. In fact, Carly's friend, Marta, owns this theater."

"Yeah?" Uh-oh. She'd obviously lost him again.

"Yes, remember I told you that Marta wants to have a memorial concert for Holly?" She turned to me. "I think it's a wonderful idea and so does Maury."

He nodded absently.

"Nice meeting you," I tried again. "I'd better get to . . ." I couldn't think of an excuse. I hated when my brain went on vacation and left my body in a delicate social situation. Ironically, Ruth saved me.

"I was just seeing Maurice out. He's staying at a condo down the street." She practically pushed him out the door. "Remember what we talked about, Maury. I'll see you tonight." He obediently left, and Ruth turned to me as if we were best buds.

"I need to talk to you," she said in a low, riveting voice. My ears stood at attention. "I called Maurice." She waited for my response. I had no idea what she was after. Thanks? Congratulations? A medal? It seemed a normal thing to me. Her sister died, Maurice was an old friend and ex, so she called him. Where's the mystery? I must have looked blank — not difficult, since I was.

She frowned as if maybe I was a little simple. "To help me figure things out."

"Things?"

She nodded emphatically and leaned toward me, her no-nonsense salt-and-pepper bob covering her face slightly. "Buck did it," she whispered.

# 8

A fortune made by a lying tongue is a
fleeting vapor and a deadly snare.
PROVERBS 21:6

I pulled back and looked into Ruth's swollen eyes. "Have you told the police?" First Joey, then Ruth. My friend, John, who also happened to be Lake View's police chief, would have been so proud of me for encouraging everyone to take their information to the police.

"Oh, yes. I told them that Buck killed her and they know about the life insurance, but as far as the other, what's to tell until we have proof?"

Life insurance I understood. But "other"? I felt like I was in a cell phone commercial. Talk about a bad connection.

"But when Maurice checks it out, we'll take the information right to the detectives. The important thing is I know Buck is the murderer."

She could be right, but my gut feeling was that — even though he was a slimeball — he wasn't a murderer. For one thing, he was coming from the other direction right after I found Holly. So unless he killed her, left the scene, then wandered back by, my money was on Reagan. I wanted to be diplomatic, but judging from her remarks when she and Holly were arguing, Ruth was aware of the relationship between Reagan and Buck.

"What about Reagan? Do you think it's possible she did it?"

"You mean because she was having an affair with Buck?" So much for being subtle.

"Well, they weren't very discreet, were they? Even I could tell they were close, but did Holly know?"

"She never admitted it if she did. You know how she is — was. It would have been nearly impossible for her to believe that her husband could prefer anyone over her." She looked so miserable and wrung out, my heart twisted.

"Do you want a cup of coffee?" I asked and motioned toward the two overstuffed lobby chairs near the smaller fireplace. I had nowhere I had to be for another couple of hours. If I couldn't spare time for someone who was grieving, what kind of person was I?

After ten minutes of listening to Ruth talk about Holly, I almost regretted my impulsive invitation. Now that she was dead, Holly had suddenly transformed into Mother Teresa to hear her sister tell it.

"She did have a certain presence," I said gently.

Ruth seemed to realize that she'd been canonizing her sister. "Well, I know she had flaws, but that wasn't really her fault. When she was growing up, we always treated her like a fragile princess. Because to us, she was. She was so beautiful and perfect that we felt like she deserved whatever she wanted. So she took it as her due, whether it belonged to someone else or not."

"I can see how that could happen." The Bible warned against spoiling children for a reason. Because if you did, they were . . . spoiled. Like something ruined.

Ruth leaned forward. "She made enemies, you know," she whispered.

I made a noncommittal sound and bit back the "You don't say?" that desperately wanted to pop out.

"But she was so gullible," Ruth continued. "She couldn't ever see possible evil. Like her stalker."

Curiosity kicked in. Hard. "Stalker?"

Ruth nodded, still staring off into the distance, as if I were invisible. "He came to at least ten shows every year — for the last three years. He sends — sent — her letters planning how they would go away together."

"Did the police know?"

"I tried to get her to go to the police when she got the first letter, but she laughed in my face. Still, there was something about those letters that gave me the creeps. Holly said he just wanted attention."

"So she encouraged him?"

Ruth frowned, and I thought I'd gone too far. But she slowly drifted back into her lazy monologue. "One show, after about a year or so of the letters, he described what he would be wearing. When Holly spotted him in the audience, she waved at him. Thought she was being cute." She pursed her lips, obviously remembering Holly's reaction. "I told her she was playing with fire. But she said if he was gonna do something, he would have done it by then. I guess she was right."

"Umm, when did she get the last letter from him?" Casual tone, but my heart was thumping.

"Just before we left Nashville. That was odd, because he usually sent the letter to the show location. But this was really just a note. It said something like, 'I've always wanted to see Branson. Maybe we can see it together.' And that was it."

"Did you tell the police about that note?"

Suddenly Ruth seemed to come out of her trance. She straightened and gave me a hard stare, almost as if she were accusing me of forcing her confidence. "I told them all they need to know. I mentioned the stalker, but I know Buck did it and that's what I told them." She stood, her back as straight as if she had a rod for a backbone. The slumped, helpless woman was gone. I had a feeling that was the last information I would get from Ruth.

As she strode out of the lobby, I remained where I was, transfixed by the extreme sudden change in her. One thought gripped me. Was there really a stalker? Or was he just a made-up scapegoat in case Buck managed to prove his innocence? Ruth obviously loved her sister, but she also had plenty of reasons to hate her. What if she'd pulled the same Dr. Jekyll/Mr. Hyde Saturday night as she had just now and killed Holly?

"Poor Ruth. It can't have been easy living in Holly's shadow." Marta took a sip of her tea.

"The bane of talentless sisters every-where," Carly intoned dryly as she leaned forward to offer John another piece of grilled trout.

"Tell me about it." I held up my last bite of fish. "I'm not the one who made us a gourmet meal out of a morning's catch."

"Now that you mention it . . ." she drawled. "You're looking a little pale. Must be all that time in my shadow."

I touched my sunburned face. "Make fun of me, why don't you?"

Hayley looked up from her plate. "Aunt Jenna, why didn't you wear sunscreen?"

"Yeah," Rachel piped up. "You're always telling us to."

I smiled. "Extenuating circumstances."

She gave me a puzzled glance then looked at her mom.

Carly pursed her lips and shook her head. "Aunt Jenna got distracted. But see how she paid for it?"

"So who all is still staying in the hotel?" I asked, partly to divert attention from my sunburned face and partly because I was curious. "I know Buck left Sunday." I'd told Marta and Carly about his request. Unfortunately, every time I started to clean out the room, something kept me from it. There was no telling what clues were in there.

Waiting. "And Ruth left today, didn't she?"

"Yes, she went to Nashville for the reading of the will," Marta said. "Joey and Reagan are still here."

"Really?" Carly's brows drew together. "Wonder why?"

"Apparently the police aren't quite ready for either of the guitar players to leave town, so I told them they could stay for a while longer." Marta must have seen the surprised look we exchanged, because she hurried on. "Both of them offered to work for their room and board. As a matter of fact, Reagan got wind somewhere of the memorial concert plans and volunteered to sing."

Carly snorted. "I can just see Ruth going along with that."

I nodded. "It doesn't seem very likely."

The twins pushed their empty plates away, apparently bored with the adult conversation. Rachel looked at her mom. "Supper was great."

"Can we go, please?" Hayley asked.

Carly hesitated, and again I thought of how differently we reacted since the murder. When we first arrived, Paradise Theater and Hotel seemed like the safest place in the world. "You may be excused from the table, but you can't go back to our suite without us," Carly said firmly.

They shoved to their feet, and Zac and Dani did the same.

"Hold it right there." They turned to look at Carly. "Plates in the sink."

They groaned, but all four of them carried their plates and silverware into the kitchen before disappearing into the living room.

Marta looked at Carly. "I guess we know who needs to be in charge of getting the memorial concert together."

"Me?" Carly squeaked. "Not unless you're havin' the concert in a kitchen, sugar."

"If that's the only way you'll help, we might consider it," John deadpanned.

Marta cut her gaze to him. "I thought we were going to ease into it."

He chuckled. "That's as subtle as I could be while begging for help, honey."

Marta blew out an outraged breath. "John! I never said to beg —"

Carly and I exchanged a quick look. "Y'all don't have to beg us. We'll help any way we can," she said.

Marta set her napkin on the table and pulled a sheet of paper from her pocket. "I agree that Ruth would never go along with letting Reagan sing, so I need you two to call these country singers and see if any of them are willing to perform at the tribute."

Carly took the paper. "Y'all asked Buck about speaking?"

"Yes, he agreed *and* offered to let us use a short video montage he's having done of Holly."

"What about Ruth? Will she say a few words?" I couldn't imagine her onstage, but based on what I'd seen earlier, there could be a superstar personality lurking inside her mousy exterior.

"She asked if Maurice could speak in her place. Buck wasn't thrilled about it, but he couldn't really say no. So that's what we're doing."

"That's great, Marta." Carly handed me the sheet.

I glanced at the list. These were the biggest names in country music. "Did you decide to charge admission?"

John cleared his throat. "Well, I —"

"No!" Marta jumped to her feet. "I told you I don't want to profit from her death."

John dropped his fork onto his plate. "Listen, honey —"

Her eyes flashed. "Don't you 'honey' me."

"Marta," he said softly. "Believe me, we're not going to 'profit' from her death. I was just hoping we could make back a little of what her death cost us."

Tears sparkled in her eyes and she sat back

down. "I'm sorry. I just wanted to do something nice for Holly." She nodded toward the list. "I know it's a long shot. But I was hoping someone on that list might sing Holly's songs just as a tribute to her. Not for the money."

"If we could find a singer who would do that . . ." Carly mused. "Then you could take donations at the door and recoup some of your losses." She gave Marta a shrewd look. "*Without* charging admission."

"It's really short notice, though." I hated to be the voice of reason, but the chances of any of those names not being already booked for two weeks from Friday were slim to none. Marta's lips tilted down. "But we'll try."

Marta sighed. "How much longer can you stay?"

Before Carly had a chance to commit us to hanging around Branson until the concert, I spoke up. I had a cat and a dog, not to mention a lawyer, who missed me. "We should probably head home Friday afternoon. That way I can go back to work on Monday and take more time off when we come back for the concert."

"Sounds perfect," John boomed.

"It does." Marta pushed to her feet. "Thank y'all so much. Who wants coffee?"

"Definitely me." Carly started clearing the table.

"I'd better not. I've got . . . things I need to do." I said good night to John and Marta. "My compliments to both the chef and the hosts."

"Dear Pru?" Carly mouthed as John and Marta carried things into the kitchen.

I nodded.

"See you back at the suite later, then."

As I stepped out into the hot, humid night, a strange noise drifted to me. I followed the stepping-stones around to the sidewalk in front of the hotel and suddenly realized what it was.

Singing.

Holly's fans. I slowly walked toward them, drawn by the a cappella singing and the sea of candles swaying in the darkness. Were these the same people who had been out here since the murder? Or were they taking the vigil in shifts?

As I eased up to the group, the first thing that struck me was how normal they all looked. A mother wearing a T-shirt proclaiming, *God Needed a Perfect Angel So He Took Holly* clutched her preteen's hand. I frowned. Several others were wearing the same shirt. As conscientious as Marta was about not making money off Holly's death, others obviously had no such compunction.

A college-age boy stood behind his tearful girlfriend, his arms wrapped around her as she waved a candle. She glanced at me and pressed her lips together as new tears poured down her face.

Her grief pained me and I turned away. Into a face distorted with rage. His hate-filled gaze burned into mine, and his lips were drawn into a snarl.

I stumbled back. A group of middle-aged women shifted into the gap between us. Without looking back, I sprinted for the front door of the hotel. I ignored the startled desk clerk and continued to run until I reached our suite.

Behind the safety of my locked door, I collapsed against the wall and slid down to the floor. I picked at the gray tweed of the carpet, my heart pounding in my ears. I'd seen people angry before. And the man didn't seem to be mad at me personally, but just filled with rage. So why had his anger chilled me to the bone? Before the question formed in my mind, I knew the answer. I was afraid I'd stepped directly into the path of a murderer.

# 9

A gossip betrays a confidence; so avoid a
man who talks too much.

PROVERBS 20:19

I sat on the floor and prayed for at least ten
minutes. When I stood, I was considerably
calmer, but I still knew that if hate had a
face, that man's was it. I wanted to call the
police. But what would I tell them? That I
had a bad feeling about one of Holly's fans?
That he seemed to be disproportionately
angry? That didn't even make sense. I might
as well just tell them a good joke. I'd get
the same laughs.

Just as I reached for the Dear Pru files,
my cell phone rang. For a split second, I
was afraid to look at the caller ID and even
more afraid to answer it. I shook my head
and looked at the number. Alex.

"Hey!"

"Hey, water girl. Or should I say Detective Stafford?"

I laughed. Shakily. "I'll just stick with Jenna. The last thing I'm interested in tonight is investigating Holly's murder."

"What happened?" His voice grew quickly serious. "Are you okay?"

I told him about the man outside, relieved to be able to share my fear with someone I knew wouldn't think I was crazy.

"Come home."

That was love in his voice, wasn't it?

"I can't. We promised Marta and John that we'd help with the memorial concert. It's in two weeks."

"You're planning on staying for two weeks?" He sounded panicked.

I felt better. "No. Just a few more days for now. We'll be home Friday night."

"Why don't I come back up there until then?"

"Alex, listen. I promise to be careful. If this man is the murderer, the police will find him. He's right out in the front of the hotel. He's probably been out there since the news broke about her death. Maybe he's just hurt and angry that she's gone and isn't a threat at all."

"Maybe. But you still need to be careful."

"I will, Alex." I tossed the Dear Pru files onto the bed. "I'm glad you made it home.

I've got some things I've got to do, so I'd better go."

"Okay. Will you be home in time for us to go out Friday night?"

"Sure, I'd love to."

"Good." He hesitated. "Well, I'll let you go. Take care, Jenna."

My lips twisted in a bittersweet smile. "You, too."

I flipped the phone shut and picked up the first Dear Pru letter.

My boyfriend of two years is the man of my dreams. Really. But I think he's become obsessed with me. He frequently tells me he loves me and gets upset if I don't respond. My best friend says I should be grateful that he's open about his feelings. But I'm not so sure. What do you think?

I tossed the letter onto the bed and grabbed my gown from the drawer. Maybe tomorrow I'd feel like giving this poor soul some sound advice. Right now I just wanted to give her a sound whack on the side of the head with a verbal two-by-four. Just because someone needed to hear "I love you" didn't mean they were obsessed. Did it?

■ ■ ■ ■

The next morning, I was half finished with my swim when Detective Jamison walked in. I wasn't in the mood to be scared off this time, so I completed my laps, studiously ignoring him.

After I finished, I quickly showered and dressed. I thought I'd be sitting at Starbucks working on Dear Pru letters before the detective got out of the pool. But when I came out of the women's locker room, he was coming from the men's, fully dressed. Either he'd cut his workout short or I'd taken a longer shower than I thought.

A loud *crash* outside drew my gaze to the floor-to-ceiling windows around the pool. Lightning flashed. Rain suddenly pounded down, blowing hard against the glass.

No way I was going out in that downpour. Starbucks and Dear Pru could wait. I plopped my gym bag on the small table, sat down in a white plastic chair, my back to the floor-to-ceiling windows, and stared at the concrete block wall.

"Olympics, huh? That must have been pretty exciting." A crash of thunder punctuated his bombshell.

He slid into the chair next to me as if I'd

invited him.

"If you consider letting down your home-town and possibly your whole country before you're even old enough to vote, then sure. It was a bundle of excitement." I slipped my fingers through my gym bag handle and scooted it toward me.

"So you're embarrassed? That's why you lied to me about having professional training?"

"I didn't lie! I said I'm not in professional training now. Two entirely different things."

"I see."

My knuckles whitened on the gym bag handle. "And I'm not embarrassed. I'm just being realistic about the experience."

His smile seemed genuine, not snarky like I'd have expected. And it softened his whole face. "Isn't it funny how we always focus on the negative and forget the good parts?"

"What good parts?" The loudness of the rain threatened to drown out my voice.

He leaned forward. "I'm sure there had to be a great feeling of accomplishment when you made the Olympic team."

I shrugged. But as soon as he said it, I did remember how excited I'd been.

"Maybe you've forgotten how great you must have felt just knowing you'd made it there?"

Tears pricked at my eyes. I blinked. "Maybe." If I was honest with myself, I knew I had. The end result had seemed so catastrophic that I had blocked out the thrill of going. But I wasn't going to admit it to a stranger. "Did you want to be in the Olympics? You're a very good swimmer."

He frowned and motioned toward the pool. "I took up swimming after my wife died five years ago. So I was way too old for Olympic aspirations. Unless there's such a thing as the Senior Citizen Olympics."

"I don't think you qualify for those, Detective." My best guess at his age would be forty-five.

"Call me Jim."

I looked up, startled that he'd want to be on first-name basis with me.

As if he read my mind, he said, "May I call you Jenna?"

I nodded. "So you preferred to get your fame by solving murders?"

He laughed. "Not everyone wants fame. Was that really why you wanted to be in the Olympics?"

"Actually that was my least favorite part."

"That's what I would have guessed." He looked out the window as if fascinated by the rain. "Your friend Holly seemed to thrive on her fame."

"She did. But she wasn't my friend. It was more of a servant-master relationship." I kind of laughed then stopped when he looked at me intently. "I mean, Marta asked us to come here to help her take care of Holly." But he already knew that.

"Ah, yes, Marta and Holly were high school friends, weren't they?"

I snorted. "Holly wasn't the type to have female friends."

"Really? I would think all the girls would want to be her friend. Unless they were jealous?" For someone who was so perceptive a minute ago, he didn't seem all that intuitive now.

"Like I said, Holly didn't make friends. She made groupies." I tried not to sound negative since I didn't want to be at the top of the suspect list.

"Well, Marta and your sister were close, weren't they?"

Finally, a subject I was more comfortable with. "Yes, they've been best friends as long as I can remember. They stayed friends even after they married."

"The Hills seem to have a good relationship."

"Yep. Marta always says they're the perfect balance. He's easygoing, the voice of reason, and she's impulsive and quick-tempered."

"Really?"

Had I lost my mind? I just told the chief detective in charge of Holly's murder case that Marta had a bad temper.

"Well, not quick-tempered maybe. Just impulsive and sometimes she gets a little aggravated, then quickly gets over it."

He was staring at me as if he were reading my thoughts again. I wanted to add, "She would never kill anyone, though." But even I had sense enough to know that would make things worse.

"Have you seen her ever do anything violent when she was mad?"

I frowned. "No. You can forget Marta. She didn't kill Holly."

"And you know this because . . . ?"

"Because she wouldn't hurt a fly. Maybe you should find out why Joey hated Holly. And what he was doing in her suite Sunday while Buck was at the station. And while you're at it, you might consider that I found Reagan hiding in Holly's dressing room closet. Marta is the least —"

His eyes bored into mine. "What were you doing in Holly's dressing room?"

Too late I remembered the crime scene tape. Me and my big mouth. I clamped my lips together and resisted the urge to turn an imaginary key and throw it away.

The only sound was the pounding of rain.

Finally he leaned toward me. "Jenna, I get the feeling you've taken an interest in this crime. My guess is you read mystery novels, and now you think you're the next Miss Marple. But you'd do well to remember those are books. In real life if you mess with a murderer, you'll probably end up dead."

I dropped my gaze to the table.

He cleared his throat, and I looked up.

"And that would be a real shame."

I jumped to my feet.

"I can't wait any longer. I've got things to do," I stammered. " 'Bye." I clutched my bag to my chest and dashed out into the torrential rain. I was reminded of my sprint to get away from the fanatic last night. Considering my innocence, I sure did seem to spend a lot of time running away these days.

I'd dried out completely by midafternoon. Fueled by white chocolate lattés, I'd even finished the Dear Pru letters. When I got back to our suite, the first thing I saw was a note on my bed.

*At Marta's. Come over when you get in.*
$\sim$ *C*

I made my way to Marta's via the back entrance this time. I didn't want to go near the mourners out front. Not after last night. I knocked and waited then knocked again. Finally Zac opened the door. "Mom's in the kitchen." He disappeared into the living room, where I could hear a DVD trivia game playing. I stood in the foyer for a minute and breathed in the spicy aroma of cinnamon rolls mixed with the warm nutty smell of banana nut bread. Yum. But uh-oh.

I rushed into the kitchen. The empty kitchen. "Carly?"

She popped up from behind the work space. "Jenna, I'm so glad you're here. I didn't want to call you because I knew you needed to work."

Flour spotted her face, but it was easy to see her eyes were swollen and red. "What happened?"

"They've taken Marta away."

Okay. They. The little men in white coats? Aliens from outer space? The city zoning board? Well, my boss had been having trouble with our zoning board, so it's not as far-fetched as it sounded. I waited for en-lightenment.

"They think she had something to do with the murder." Carly looked at me as if I were obtuse, which I probably was. But I finally knew who *they* were.

"The *police* took her?"

"Yes. That's what I've been telling you."

"Why did they take her? What did they say?" Suddenly I remembered what I'd said to Jim — Detective Jamison just a few short hours ago. Was I responsible for Marta being arrested?

"They just said they needed her for more questioning. She asked what it was about, and they said they'd discuss it at the station."

"Did John go with her?"

"Oh, yeah. He had to. Marta was so upset when she called me." She looked toward the living room. "The kids were at our suite when it happened. They think John and Marta just went to town for something." Her voice broke. "Poor Dani."

"Wait. She wasn't actually arrested, right?"

"Not officially. They let John drive her. But who knows what's happened by now?"

The *click* of the front door opening drew us both out of the kitchen. Marta looked at us bleakly. Behind her, John's always-pleasant face was a thundercloud. Not good signs.

"Marta," Carly whispered, glancing toward the living room where the kids thankfully had the volume on their game set to loud. "I can't believe they took you in for questioning. They should be able to tell by looking at you that you wouldn't hurt a flea."

I waited for Marta to explode the way she often did when I made her mad as a kid. No explosion. She just walked toward the kitchen looking defeated. What was going on?

"John?" Carly said, her voice trembling.

He ran his hand over his thinning hair and motioned for us to precede him into the kitchen. "Marta and Holly had a fuss. Someone overheard it and reported it to the police."

Marta was sitting on a stool, elbows on the bar, chin in her hands. "Holly started being difficult," she said softly.

Apparently she wasn't out of it enough not to see the look that Carly and I exchanged, because she sighed. "Okay, *more* difficult. She got more and more demanding — insisting after the first night that we cut the intermission." She glanced up at us, indignation flaring in her eyes. "Do you know how much we make on concessions? But we had no choice but to go along with her or she'd leave."

"I don't understand," Carly said, sinking onto the stool next to Marta. "Didn't Holly have a contract?"

"Yes, but her agent called the day of the

147

opening show to tell her she had an offer to play a huge venue. They were offering twice as much as we were. She wanted out of her contract. I refused. From that moment on, I think she set out to make me want to get rid of her."

Her face paled. "Not get rid of her, get rid of her. I mean let her out of her contract." She leaned closer to Carly. "At that point I would have loved nothing better than to see the last of her." She gasped. "No wonder the police suspect me. Nothing I say comes out right."

Carly patted her shoulder. "With Buck and Ruth both in Nashville for the reading of the will, the detectives probably just had some time on their hands. We know you didn't kill Holly. And I'm sure they do, too."

"I hope you're right. We'd have been ruined if she left. It was too late to line up another act, and we had sold tickets." She looked at John then took a deep breath as if she'd decided to tell the whole truth. "We'd already used the money to refurbish the theater. I knew we'd be knee-deep in trouble if Holly left." Marta gave a bitter laugh. "I was sure right about that."

"But for that very reason, it makes no sense that they'd suspect you," I said. "You had the most to lose by Holly being out of the picture." Unless they thought she did it in a fit of temper. Guilt churned in my stomach. Why hadn't I just stayed completely out of that conversation with Detective Jamison? I'd let my guard down with him because he'd been so insightful and understanding about the Olympics. But at what cost?

Thursday morning, I went late to the pool, with one purpose in mind. My timing was perfect. I'd barely walked in the door when Detective Jamison came out of the men's locker room, fully dressed.

"Good morning," he said, his deep voice cheerful.

I glared at him.

"Or not?"

"Yeah, right," I snarled. "You don't have a clue why I might be in a bad mood."

He raised his eyebrows.

"You used me. You took advantage of our relaxed conversation to get me to say something against my friend then brought her in for questioning."

He stepped toward me. "Actually . . ." He lowered his voice in a very cloak-and-dagger way. "Marta was already on the list to be brought in based on that overheard argument between her and the victim. Our

149

conversation had nothing to do with it."

"Honestly?"

He nodded.

My sigh of relief was cut short when he chuckled. "Not that I'm above using information from any source to solve a case."

"I see. Thanks for the heads up." Forewarned was forearmed, so I'd be keeping my mouth firmly shut in the future.

"Jenna, don't you want the murderer brought to justice, even if it is your friend?"

Did I? I frowned. "Marta didn't kill her."

"Unlike amateurs, real investigators start out with no preconceptions." He swept out the door without another word.

But he'd planted a seed that I couldn't unplant, no matter how much I wanted to. The whole time I swam, unwelcome memories tumbled through my brain. Marta telling Holly that she'd be on that stage Friday night or else. Marta adamantly refusing to profit from Holly's death. At the end of my workout, I was no closer to answering the terrible question — was the very person we were trying to help actually the killer?

# 10

A gentle answer turns away wrath, but a harsh word stirs up anger.

PROVERBS 15:1

When I got back to the suite, Marta was waiting in our sitting room.

Guilt hit me hard when I saw her. What had I been thinking?

Marta smiled and held up a bag of black garbage bags. "You're gonna kill me."

I ignored her unfortunate turn of phrase and smiled. "What's up?"

"I'm here asking for a favor again. I was hoping you and Carly would help me gather up the teddy bears and candles the wind scattered all across the front of our property. Thankfully, the Branson chapter of Holly's fan club took most of them right before the storm yesterday morning, but I think it must have started raining before they finished."

I remembered the fanatic from the other night. "Are the mourners gone?"

She nodded.

"Sure, I'll help."

"I knew I could count on you. I don't know what we'd have done without you and Carly."

Carly came bounding out of the bedroom in tennis shoes, jeans, and an old T-shirt. "We've had a good time."

I cut my gaze at her. A good time?

She shrugged behind Marta's back with a "What was I supposed to say?" expression.

"It's been an adventure," I said. "And we're always up for an adventure."

"Did you tell Jenna the news?" Carly asked.

I glanced at Marta. "What news?"

Marta looked back over her shoulder as she started out the door.

"I called Buck to see if he could be here tomorrow night for a planning meeting for the memorial concert. He said he'd be here for the concert and help any way he could in the planning, but that he wouldn't be at the meeting."

I pulled the door behind us with a *click.* "He must have his hands full, getting things ready for the funeral."

Carly shook her head. "Not according to

him. He said that Ruth is in charge of the funeral. And everything else."

I lowered my voice as we passed the other suites. "Everything else?"

Marta nodded. "Apparently Holly left Buck out of the will."

That wasn't such a surprise, really. "I remember Ruth saying he signed a prenup, so maybe —"

Carly butted in. "So then Marta called Ruth, and she's going to be here tomorrow night. But you'll never guess where the funeral is going to be."

Apparently not in Nashville or it wouldn't be a surprise. How many times had Carly and Marta tag teamed me with their guessing games? Too many to count over the years. Personally, I think they just liked to see me guess wrong. "Here?"

"Hardly." Carly pushed open the outside door. "Ruth chose a venue much more intimate."

"You might want to press your little black dress, Jenna," Marta said as she tossed me a garbage bag. "The funeral is in Lake View."

I skidded to a stop. "Lake View, Arkansas?"

"I know. Can you believe it?" Carly waited for Marta to tear off a black bag for her. "Our little hometown won't know what hit it."

We spread out and began to gather the soggy stuffed bears and bunnies, along with candles and wet, unreadable notes of devotion.

As I stuffed my bag, I was suddenly seized by a deep pity for Holly. She'd had so many admirers, but she hadn't gotten along with her sister, couldn't hold a husband, and, even with constant positive reinforcement, hadn't been happy.

Carly wasn't far away, and I looked over at her. "Why do you think Ruth set the funeral in Lake View?"

She looked up at me. "Just a guess, but maybe she's passive-aggressive and thought she'd finally get back at Holly for all the mean things she said and did to her?"

"Maybe she really thought Holly would prefer to be buried near their parents," I mused, hoping I was right.

"Ha. You and I both know Holly would have wanted a giant tombstone right in the middle of Nashville. Maybe with an eternal flame and plenty of room for the fans who would make their annual trek there to pay homage to the late queen."

"Yeah, you're probably right." I snagged a letter plastered against the base of Paul Bunyan's guitar. Somehow the rain hadn't defaced it enough to make it illegible. "I love you, I love you, I love you" was written on every inch of the page. I rested for a second on the stone base and stared at the words. Which was better? Those words repeated mindlessly? Or an obviously caring action like driving to Branson to check on me? Had I gotten so hung up on hearing Alex say those three little words that I'd lost sight of what love really was?

"Have you seen Marta?" Carly yelled.

I shook my head, and we both turned toward the area near the building where Marta had been cleaning.

"She was there a minute ago," I said.

Carly frowned then ran around to the other side of the building. I followed her at a slower pace.

"Turn her loose!" Carly screamed as I rounded the corner. Like a mini-tornado, she headed toward the man who was pulling a struggling Marta into the woods.

"Back off if you want her alive," a harsh voice snarled.

I froze, my heart pounding. His hair was dank and twisted, and he looked like he hadn't slept or eaten in days, but the burning eyes were the same. My nightmare from Monday night's crowd was back. And he had his arm locked around Marta's neck.

"She hasn't done anything to you." Carly's

voice, though a little trembly and out of breath, was that of a mother soothing a frightened child. "She won't hurt you. We're just cleaning up so it will look nice. That's what Holly would want."

He didn't relax his hold.

"I don't care what you do. It's too late to help my sweet Holly. We had such plans." He shook an already shaking Marta, and I was afraid he'd snap her neck. "But thanks to you, we'll never get to carry them out."

It hit me as surely as if Paul Bunyan's guitar had fallen on me. This was the stalker Ruth had told me about.

"I didn't do anything," Marta croaked.

"You own this place, don't you?"

"Yes," she admitted.

"If you'd had good security, no one could've gotten to Holly. You didn't even have a security camera up. Anyone could get in without being seen."

"How do you know that?" I wondered aloud.

His brow wrinkled as if the distraction puzzled him. When his face wasn't distorted with anger, I could see that at one time, he'd been fairly nice-looking. But despair and grief had taken their toll. Not to mention a touch of craziness. It had been just two days since I ran into him Monday night, and he looked so much worse than he had then.

"I have security cameras. They're just not up yet. Holly wouldn't let me have them installed," Marta stammered. "She said they made her nervous. I begged her to allow it, but that was one of her stipulations."

"Trying to blame someone who's not here to defend herself?" His dirty hair hung in his eyes. He slung his head back and pushed Marta onto her knees. "You had the most precious person in the world to guard and you failed."

"How can you say that? Marta did everything a person could do to make sure Holly was safe and happy." Carly was no longer trying to soothe. She was furious.

I put my hand on her arm, because for a second I thought she was going to take her chances and tackle him.

"Everything except take the precautions anyone with sense would take." He shifted his weight but never loosened his death grip on Marta's neck. "Saturday morning, Holly let me in and assured me no one would know. I asked her then about security cams, and she said you were too cheap to install them."

He sounded like he was telling the truth. And if this was the same stalker, Ruth had said Holly was convinced he was harmless. "Holly let you in?"

"You got a problem with that?" He glared at me. "For your information, Holly and I were like that." In front of Marta's face, he twined two fingers together. "I would have taken care of her. She knew that. Not like El Cheapo here."

"He's right." The words were whispered, the tone defeated.

He loosened his grip a little, and Marta pushed to her feet, craning around to look in his face. "You're right. I should've had security cams in place, no matter what Holly said. But she barely allowed me to have guards. And she wouldn't let me put them anywhere close to her room. She said it made her feel trapped." For the first time since the ordeal started, tears coursed down Marta's cheeks.

The stalker relaxed his grip some, and Marta turned completely to face him.

"She did tell me that." Something in his voice had changed. I looked closer. His own eyes were filled with tears.

Marta stepped back out of his grasp, seemingly without a struggle. "I'm so sorry. Nothing you can say can make me feel worse than I already feel."

Sobbing, the man turned and walked into

the trees without a backward glance.

Marta collapsed into Carly's arms, and I quickly called 911.

Branson's finest arrived almost immediately. I'd been worried that they'd doubt our story since Marta had just been taken in for questioning, but the officers obviously took the threat seriously. They were still combing the woods when Detective Jamison arrived. The officer nearest me filled him in on the situation.

"Are you ladies okay?" he asked, concern evident in his voice.

We nodded. He asked us a few more questions, and with each of us filling in the blanks, we were able to tell him the whole conversation verbatim. When the security cameras were mentioned, a glance passed between him and Marta that told me this topic had come up before.

An officer came out of the woods and approached us. "We found tire tracks on a back road where a car had apparently been parked. Our guess is that the suspect parked there and walked over."

"Then ran back to his car to make his getaway," Detective Jamison added, nodding. "He's long gone by now."

He handed us each a card. "If you think of anything you haven't told me, please call."

"We will," Marta said shakily. She didn't seem to have any hard feelings over his questioning her yesterday.

Carly put her arm around her friend and guided her to the front door.

I turned back to Detective Jamison. "I appreciate your department responding so quickly. And thanks for taking the threat seriously."

He smiled. "It's like I told you this morning. A good investigator doesn't have preconceived notions about who's guilty and who's not."

"Yeah, I'm keeping that in mind."

"Actually, I don't want you to worry about that. I just want you to call me if you see or hear anything suspicious. No amateur sleuthing. Just call me, okay?" I didn't say anything, and he touched my arm. "That old saying about curiosity killing the cat has more than a grain of truth."

I couldn't believe it. My mama had used that saying against me my whole life. Now a cop in another state was doing it. "It's lucky a cat has nine lives then, so he can live to be curious another day."

His jaw tightened. "Stay out of this murder investigation, Jenna. Consider that an official warning."

■ ■ ■ ■

My hand shook as I slid the key card down the slot. The green light flashed and the door opened smoothly, but in my mind it creaked mysteriously. I closed it firmly, and yes, quietly, behind me, letting the scent of expensive perfume settle over me like a mantle before I turned and surveyed the territory. I slid the key back into my pocket. Sanctioned snooping felt so odd.

I easily found the suitcases and bags at the back of the walk-in closet. The rows of hanging clothes astounded me. How many outfits could one person wear? I filled one garment bag after another with hanging clothes then slid them into a tall suitcase, obviously made for that purpose.

Holly's custom-designed luggage made it easy to see which one was for shoes, and it didn't take me long to get the seemingly endless collection stored away. One thing about it: If Bob didn't sell the athletic club to me soon, I could always look into a new career as personal assistant to the stars.

By the time I finished the closet and prepared to tackle the drawers, I'd changed my mind. I'd stick to Dear Pru and look for something similar if my day job fell through.

Buck was a smooth operator. I would have earned every penny of the Benjamin Franklin I'd refused and possibly more. And so far I'd found nothing but a few notes from fans. Nothing beyond the usual "You're my favorite singer" or "I'd love an autographed picture" and a startling number that were variations of "Will you marry me?"

A loud knock on the door made me dive behind the bed. I admit I even lifted the comforter up to see if I could climb under the bed if I needed to, but there were boards going all the way to the floor. Another knock.

"Jenna? Are you in there?"

My sister. I jumped up and ran to open the door. I grabbed Carly's arm and pulled her inside. "What are you doing here?" I hissed.

She narrowed her eyes and gave a little shake of her head as if I were crazy. "I came to help you. I told you I would if Marta was resting."

"I thought you'd call me. Not bang on the door and scream my name."

"I didn't scream your name!" she screamed.

"Shh . . ."

"What's your problem? Correct me if I'm wrong, but didn't Buck ask you to pack this stuff up and ship it home?"

"Yes." I sank onto the couch.

"And didn't you call Ruth this morning and ask her if she wanted you to and she said yes, please?"

"Yes."

"You seriously need to get a grip. Every errand isn't a covert operation."

"Fine," I said tight-lipped, but I knew she was right. "Let's get to packing."

She tossed me a saucy grin. "You're welcome, sugar. It was my pleasure to come help you."

A smile tipped the corners of my mouth. "Thank you."

"That's more like it."

I opened the top drawer and Carly said, "Whoa, baby."

Holly apparently owned stock in a lingerie company.

Carly reached in and with two fingers lifted out a tiny black nightgown. She shook her head and dropped it into the suitcase. Then she carefully extracted a red one that was mostly lace.

"That'll take all day." I scooped out the contents of the drawer and transferred the whole armload to the suitcase. "There. That's settled."

She pulled the next drawer open. "Oh, my

goodness. I bet she only opened this drawer when Buck was out and the door was dead bolted."

"Oh, no. I'm afraid to look." In spite of my apprehension, I peeked over her shoulder. The second drawer was filled with sweatpants and hoodies.

I emptied the drawer and stacked them neatly in the suitcase. "These make Holly seem more like a real person, don't they?"

"Yeah. I bet she had a hard time ever being able to relax." Carly's eyes looked moist.

I quickly opened the third drawer. In Holly's almost compulsively neat system, the tangled pile of pantyhose stood out like a punk rocker in Branson. Especially since the pantyhose box was underneath the pile with pantyhose sticking out the opening. Weird," I murmured.

"What?" It was Carly's turn to lean over my shoulder.

"Oh, nothing." I started to stuff the hose that were lying loose in the drawer back into the pink box. My fingers touched the edge of a paper in the bottom of the box. I pulled all the nylons out and retrieved a few folded sheets of paper. I unfolded them and stared at the official bank logo at the top of each one.

I sat back cross-legged on the floor. "Why

would Holly bring bank statements with her on tour? And even more importantly, why would she hide them so carefully?"

Carly plopped down on the floor beside me. "Inquiring minds want to know."

"I know mine does." I skimmed the figures, some which were circled. "It looks about like my own bank statement, only with bigger numbers."

I handed the first page to Carly.

She nodded. "Much, much bigger numbers."

"Rub it in, why don't you?" I skimmed the second page and stopped. "Look at this."

"It looks like someone withdrew twenty thousand dollars three times that month."

"I'd think that was normal star spending, but look at the tiny question marks beside each of these transactions." I did a quick check of the other three pages and found them to be similar. The amounts withdrawn during each month varied from ten thousand to fifty thousand, but each appeared to be a cash withdrawal and each had a question mark beside it. A few times the letter *B* appeared with a question mark after it.

"That looks bad for Buck, doesn't it?" Carly said, then went to work in the bathroom without waiting for an answer.

I put the papers back into the box and set it on the dresser. The whole rest of the time we were packing up, my mind raced. Who should I give the bank statement pages to?

When Carly came out of the bathroom with a satchel packed full of toiletries, I was sitting in the Victorian armchair holding the pantyhose box. "Snooping with permission isn't all it's cracked up to be. I have no idea what to do with these."

She gave me a sympathetic nod.

"I can't imagine giving them to Buck, considering the *B* scrawled out beside half the question marks."

"No." She looked at the stuff we'd just packed. "Actually I'm not sure any of this should go to Buck now since we know what the will said."

"Great. Another dilemma."

"I didn't make it, I just pointed it out."

"Well, since Ruth is the heir apparent, I guess it all belongs to her, including the bank statements. But what if she's the killer?"

"She surely wouldn't kill her own sister." Carly looked genuinely shocked.

"Not everybody has as good a sister as you do," I joked. "Maybe if I give them to Ruth, she'll pass them on to Maurice."

"Oh, that's good thinking. As Holly's

financial advisor, he should know what to do with them. Or . . ." She grinned. "If you're feeling really brave, you could take them to Detective Jamison."

"I'm not afraid of him." Not much anyway. "But he'd just accuse me again of butting in on his investigation. I'll just give them to Ruth at our planning meeting tonight." I looked at the packed suitcases. "And talk to her about the rest of this stuff before I have it shipped to Buck."

"In that case, let's call it a morning and go get some lunch." Carly headed for the door. She looked back over her shoulder at me. "Speaking of Detective Hawk Man, should Alex be worried?"

"No!" I blurted instinctively.

She turned around and pinned me with her gaze. "That sounded a little defensive."

"It did, didn't it?" I considered the two men. "Honestly, for me, no one holds a candle to Alex."

"That's what I thought." Carly pulled the door open and motioned me to go ahead of her.

"What if the reason Alex won't commit is because he's just not that into me?" My voice sounded scared even to my own ears.

She popped me on the arm with the back of her hand. "That does it. From now on, you're banned from self-help books. He loves you. And eventually he'll gather the courage to tell you that."

I wished I could be so sure.

# 11

A quick-tempered man does foolish things, and a crafty man is hated.
PROVERBS 14:17

"Couldn't you have put that in a bag or just brought the pages?" Carly whispered, as we followed the wafting scent of coffee down the hall to the lobby.

I glanced at the pink pantyhose box in my hand. "Sorry. I didn't even think about it."

"People will stare."

"In case you haven't noticed, there are almost no people here. We're living in a huge hotel with less than ten guests."

We rounded the corner just in time to see Maurice and Ruth sit down on the small couch next to the unlit fireplace. Our hosts were nowhere to be seen.

Carly groaned. "I knew it. We shouldn't have sent the kids to Marta and John's house so early. I bet she had to fix them something to eat before she could come."

I rolled my eyes. "Marta's more like me than you in the cooking department. She might have microwaved potpies for them. How long can that take?"

"I'm goin' to leave you to your box and go check on them. Just to be sure everything's okay."

I didn't even get a chance to respond before she was gone. Ruth looked up and waved me over.

"Hi. John and Marta should be here in just a few minutes." Carly was right. They were both staring at my pink box. "Oh, I brought this to you." I thrust it in Ruth's lap, and for a second, I thought she'd let it fall to the floor.

She put one hand on top of it. "Thank you, Jenna."

"It's not a gift." Where was I when social graces were being passed out? "I found it in Holly's room when I was packing up her things. There are bank statement pages inside."

"Oh." A frown puckered her brow. "That's odd." She started to set them on the couch beside her.

"I noticed there were some notations in the margins." The second I saw their mouths drop open, I knew how it sounded. How it was, really. Mama was right. I was nosy. "I thought Maurice might know if something was wrong. I'm sorry. I didn't really mean to look at them. But when I pulled them out of the box, I instinctively . . ." I should have just mailed them anonymously to Detective Jamison. "I'm sorry."

Maurice reached over and took the box from Ruth. "I can understand your curiosity. It's not every day someone gets to find out how much money goes through a superstar's bank account in a month, is it?" He smiled. "I know we can trust you not to run to the tabloids with this information."

"You can trust me not to run anywhere with it."

"Just so you don't worry, you should know that Holly asked me to look into the withdrawals. She seemed to think Buck had his hand in the cookie jar without permission. Before I had time to really explore the possibility" — he blinked quickly and looked down at his lap — "she was gone." When he looked back up, his eyes were red-rimmed and watery. "I'll take these to Detective Jamison now that this has turned into a murder investigation."

"Wow. So Buck had a good reason to want Holly out of the way." I didn't realize I'd spoken aloud until Ruth answered.

"I told you Buck killed her. No one will listen to me, though."

"But they are watching Buck, aren't they?" If I knew the husband was the most likely culprit, surely the police did, too.

"They let him go back to Nashville." Ruth sounded bitter, and I didn't really blame her.

"Maybe they sent someone to keep an eye on him?" My question was rhetorical. How would we know? But Maurice surprised me.

"Yes, they did."

How did he know?

"I asked them point-blank about letting him go. He could be halfway to the Cayman Islands by now." The thought obviously bothered him. He clamped his mouth shut and shook his head.

John, Marta, and Carly appeared before he could expound. No one mentioned the pink box resting on the couch beside Maurice's leg. And I hoped no one ever did again. I'd embarrassed myself enough to last a lifetime.

Carly sank down next to me on the love seat. "You okay?" she mouthed as John and Marta were standing in front of us, greeting Ruth and Maurice.

I nodded. "It was a little hard to explain," I murmured, for her ears only.

"To an accountant?"

"I mean, why I looked."

"Oh." She winked at me. "Imagine that."

"Are you girls whispering about how many big stars you've lined up for the tribute?" Ruth asked.

We both looked up to see that John and Marta had each settled into a wing chair.

"Well, to be honest," Carly said, "we didn't get any firm commitments." I noticed she didn't address the whispering issue.

I stepped in before it came back up. "We spoke to a lot of personal assistants. And most all of them said, 'We'll see.' Or some variation of that." By the end of the afternoon, we'd considered just sending out a mass e-mail, but we'd promised Marta we'd call, so we'd gone through the whole list.

"We'll just plan the program, then, and fit the stars in as they RSVP." Ruth looked less upset by the setback of having no entertainers than she had by me looking at Holly's bank statements.

"There's always Reagan," Marta said softly.

"Unfortunately, that's true." Ruth scowled. "But she isn't going to be singing at my sister's memorial concert. Not after how she treated her when she was alive."

John leaned forward. "If the police catch

the murderer soon, I think the stars will be more receptive to performing at the Paradise."

"Not that it's about the Paradise." Marta stumbled over her words in her hurry to get them out. "We're not going to charge admission for the memorial concert, of course. The last thing we want is to profit from Holly's death."

John sat back in his chair, shoulders slightly slumped.

Ruth narrowed her eyes. "We most certainly will charge admission."

We all snapped to attention.

"But," Marta started, "I —"

"It's not open for debate. If you were to open this up free to the public, it would be mass pandemonium. Tickets will be one hundred dollars each."

Marta's eyes widened. "A hundred doll—"

Ruth raised her hand. "Half will go to the Paradise to make up for the money you had to reimburse for Saturday night. And half will go to St. Jude's Children's Hospital — Holly's favorite charity."

Maurice's brows drew together. "Holly had a favorite charity?"

"She does now," Ruth said dryly.

He nodded. "That sounds perfect, actually. Good idea." He patted her on the shoulder, and she lit up like downtown Branson at Christmas.

Well, well. Wouldn't it be wonderful if those two found a happy ending in the middle of all this trouble? I glanced at Ruth, so commanding seconds before, once again timid and meek. A happy ending would be very nice. Assuming Ruth wasn't a psycho killer.


"If you left anything, don't worry about it. I'll just hold it for you until you get back." Marta leaned in and gave Carly a hug. She tapped on the back window and waved at the girls, who were already settled in their seats. Then she came to the driver's window and hugged me, too.

"Where's Zac?" I looked over my shoulder at the twins.

"He said he and Dani were going for a walk before we had to leave."

I looked at Carly and started humming "Young Love."

She and Marta grinned. Why did I get the feeling they were already thinking about planning weddings and spoiling grandbabies together?

Carly shrugged. "Honk the horn and maybe they'll hear."

Just as I reached to tap the horn, a black and white patrol car pulled in the drive. Two uniformed officers got out. For a minute I had a flashback of when Zac was taken in for questioning about his boss's murder. I looked over at Carly. Her face was white.

"What are they doing here?" she whispered.

"I have no idea," Marta said. "But I guess I'd better find out."

She started toward them.

Zac and Dani rounded the corner of the theater holding hands. Zac froze in his tracks and pulled Dani to a stop. They watched the cops enter the hotel, Marta right behind them. They didn't move until I motioned Zac over.

"What's that all about?" he muttered as he and Dani approached our car.

I shrugged. "Nothing to do with us."

"But if I know your aunt, we're not leaving until we find out," Carly piped up from the seat next to me.

"Like you wouldn't be curious all the way home, too."

Girlish giggles erupted from the twins in the backseat as Zac leaned toward Dani. He glanced at them then dropped a lightning-quick kiss on her cheek. "See ya."

She waved, her face red, and went into

the hotel.

A couple of minutes later, the officers came out of the building escorting a hand-cuffed and struggling Joey.

We stared at each other. "Do we need to go back in and see why they arrested Joey?"

"No, let's just go on home. We can call Marta later and find out. Or . . ." She gave me an evil grin. "You can always call Detective Jamison and ask him what happened."

I ignored her attempt at wit and pulled out of the driveway. On Highway 76, I headed toward home. Carly watched me drive in silence for a couple of minutes. "You're dyin' to go back and see what's goin' on aren't you?"

"Admit it. So are you."

Carly laughed. "I admit it. But let me just call Marta and see if she knows anything. We don't want to be late getting home. You have a date with Alex tonight, remember?"

"You're right. And it seems like we've been gone forever. Mr. Persi and Neuro will have forgotten what I look like." I forced myself to keep driving away while Carly dialed Marta.

She talked for a few minutes then hung up and turned to me. "They didn't really come to arrest him. They just wanted to take him in for more questioning."

I frowned. "Then why the handcuffs?"

"Apparently Joey took exception with how one of the officers acted."

"And?" Carly can never get right to the point of a story.

"And Joey gave the cop a fat lip."

"Ouch. That looks bad for him."

"Yes, but look at Marta. Having a temper doesn't make him a murderer."

"I know." But like it or not, in the last ten minutes Joey had moved past Reagan, Ruth, and Buck to the top of my suspect list.

When the doorbell chimed, Mr. Persi ran in front of me, barking. The golden retriever had latched on to me the day of newspaper editor Hank Templeton's murder, and up until our trip to Branson, he'd been my constant companion. A tradition he apparently wanted to continue. Every step I took toward the door, he put himself directly in my path, barking nonstop. "You don't want me to leave you, do you, pal?"

Neuro, my somewhat neurotic cat, rubbed against my leg, as if to do her part in the "Keep Jenna home" campaign. "Come on, guys. Don't act like you weren't spoiled rotten at Stafford Cabins." According to Mama, the guests had all fallen in love with both my dog and my cat.

By the time I actually got to the front door, weaving in and out of the feline/canine obstacle course, I was laughing. I opened the door and gave Alex a rueful smile. "I think they missed me."

Alex grinned broadly. "Do we need to order in?" he yelled over Persi's sharp barks and loud whines.

"No, but maybe after supper we should just come back here and watch a movie."

"Sounds perfect."

On the way to the diner, I told him about Joey's arrest. "I'm impressed that you didn't ditch me to stay there where the excitement was," he joked.

I laughed. "Excitement isn't all it's cracked up to be. I'm glad to be home."

"I'm glad you're home, too."

"Thanks."

When we settled into our table, Debbie, bleached blond and single again, honed in on Alex like a heat-seeking missile. "What can I get for our favorite lawyer to drink tonight?" She giggled at her own non-joke.

"Lemonade," he said, keeping his gaze fixed on me. "Jenna?"

"Dr Pepper for me, please."

Debbie grunted and wrote it down. She'd been mad at me ever since she'd given me information about Hank's murder investigation in exchange for my promise that I wasn't dating Alex. How could I have known we'd start dating right after that?

She went to put in our drink order while we looked at the laminated menu. "I think I'll get the Friday night special." Alex tucked his menu behind the napkin holder and nodded toward the dry erase board on the wall.

"Fried catfish does sound good. And Alice's hush puppies . . . mmm . . . Carly offered her money for that recipe and she still wouldn't fork it over. No pun intended."

Alex laughed. "I'll slide one in my pocket and maybe you can get it analyzed for an ingredient list."

"Ohh, culinary espionage. You'd do that for me?" I drawled.

He leaned forward, a shadow of the laugh still on his face. "There's not much I wouldn't do for you."

"I bet I could think of some things."

"Oh yeah? Like what?"

*Like say you love me? Like ask me to be your wife?* I grimaced. "Like giving Mr. Persi a bath. Or clipping Neuro's toenails?"

"Couldn't I just pay a good groomer?"

"Some things can't be passed off for someone else to do."

His brows drew together. "I really think

Persi and Neuro would prefer for me to call a groomer."

Did he really think we were talking about groomers?

"Hard to believe Holly's funeral is going to be in Lake View, isn't it?" Alex said.

Before I could answer, Debbie reappeared with our drinks. "So do you think any big Nashville stars will be in town for Holly's funeral?"

I shrugged.

"You don't know?" Debbie put her hands on her hips. "Aren't you the one who found her body?"

"Yes."

"And you don't know what stars are coming?"

I tried to raise my eyebrow, but I can't, so I ended up squinting with one eye. "There wasn't a funeral guest list next to the body."

"Oh." She dropped her arms down by her sides and just looked at me. "Oh. I guess not."

Alex put his hand up in front of his mouth but not before I saw the ghost of a smile. I kicked him under the table.

Debbie shrugged. "I heard it was invitation only. Is that right?"

I resisted the urge to point out again that finding the body did not equate to making funeral plans. Instead, I just nodded.

"So I guess you're invited."

I nodded again.

She looked at Alex. "And you?"

He pulled his hand away from his mouth and shook his head.

She smiled at him as if he were staying away from the funeral just so she wouldn't feel left out. "Me either." She raised her order pad, pencil poised, her gaze fixed on him. "What can I get you tonight?"

For a minute, I thought I'd have to do without food, but Alex said, "We'll both have the special."

She winked at him and scrawled a few words on the page. "Two catfish plates coming up."

Her hips swiveled like the pendulum on a clock as she sashayed over to the window and slapped the order pad sheet down.

Alex wadded up his straw wrapper into a little ball and flicked it at me.

I caught it in my hand, with an expertise born of years of practice.

He grinned as I tossed it back. "Good to see you haven't lost your touch. So have you ever been to an invitation-only funeral?"

"I've never even heard of one until now. I guess Ruth had no choice. Holly had a lot of fans."

Debbie hurried toward us. "Your food will be right out." She balanced an empty round tray against her side. "So do you think it's just family, or will there be like a raffle or something for tickets for her fans?"

I was speechless. "You know, Debbie, it's not a concert. I think Ruth will just invite people who knew Holly."

"Well, that seems kind of selfish." She huffed off like I'd made the rules.

Alex picked up the saltshaker and examined it carefully, then did the same with the pepper. He reached for the napkin holder.

"What are you doing?"

He leaned forward. "Looking for the mic. Our table has to be bugged."

I laughed. "She does seem to come in right on cue, doesn't she?"

And just like that, she was back. "Alex, my mama's havin' some legal trouble."

"Really?" Alex was cool but polite. "Well, tell her to come on into the office and I'll see what I can do."

"I already told her. You helped me so much when I had trouble." She leaned forward, and I thought she was going to plant one on him. Instead, she just smiled and gazed deeply into his eyes. "I'm eternally grateful."

His face grew red. "Glad I could be of service."

A ringing bell dinged across the room. "Debbie!" Harvey barked. "Order up."

"I'll be bringin' my mama in to see you real soon," she called as she headed up to the window then promptly came back and set our supper on the table. Another bonus about ordering the special. No long wait for food.

After Alex blessed the food, I glanced across the room at the blond waitress. "So Debbie's a client?" I don't know why I was so surprised. His practice is in Lake View. Who did I think made up his clientele? "Oh, never mind. Lawyer-client confidentiality, I remember."

He smiled. "You handle that really well, considering." He took a bite of fish.

"Considering what?" I knew what he meant, but after Debbie's big pass at him, I was feeling a little defensive.

"Your natural . . . curiosity."

I picked at my own food. "Because I'm nosy, you mean?" Did I sound huffy?

"I don't think of it like that. Honestly. That's one of the things I love about you — your inquisitiveness about everything. In this day and age of mindless apathy, it's refreshing."

Okay, he had no problem proclaiming his love of my curiosity. And apparently from his phrasing there were other things he loved about me, as well. I wish I found comfort in that, but even though I *loved* my mailman's punctuality and friendliness — and he didn't look half bad in his uniform — I had no desire to profess my undying love for him.

He touched my hand. "You okay?"

Debbie bustled up to the table. "You two need a refill?"

"No, thanks," Alex replied without even looking up, still holding my hand.

I gave a quick shake of my head.

"Is something wrong with your food, Jenna?" Debbie pointed at my almost untouched plate.

"No." I slid my hand out from under Alex's. Obviously she wasn't going to leave as long as we were touching.

She turned back to Alex. "You just holler if you need anything. Anything, okay?" Wink, wink.

"Thank you." He answered as if he really thought she was just being a good waitress.

Finally she was gone.

He covered my hand with his again. "Now as I was asking before we were so rudely interrupted, are you okay?"

185

I nodded. I wanted to ask him where we were going in our relationship. But in my mind, commitment is like loyalty and respect — if you have to ask for it, you probably aren't really going to get it.

"Dread going back to work tomorrow?"

"I don't know. I've missed the athletic club actually." I just hadn't missed certain employees, but no need to dwell on the negative.

"I heard it's falling apart without you." He rubbed the back of my hand with his thumb and gave me a slow grin. "I can believe it."

I smiled. He might be a commitment phobe, but he was a sweet one. "I doubt it. I guess I'll find out tomorrow how true the rumors are."

We talked for a few more minutes while we finished our food; then Debbie waltzed over and tucked the check under the edge of Alex's plate. If I were a betting woman, I'd have laid odds that she'd written her phone number on it. I couldn't imagine him using it, but there were no guarantees.

When we got back to my house, the animals welcomed us at the door.

Two hours later, the credits rolled to the sweet romantic comedy, and Alex grunted and rolled over on the couch, almost knocking Mr. Persi onto the floor. Neuro raised her sleepy head as if to remind her bed to be still. She yawned and snuggled back down into the bend of his leg.

Halfway through the movie, I'd gone to fix popcorn. And when I came back I found this Dr. Doolittle scene asleep on my couch. I didn't have the heart to wake him.

But now that the movie was over, so was naptime. "Alex," I whispered as I shook his shoulder gently.

"Hmm?" he grumbled and opened one eye, then the other one. "Oh, hey. Sorry." He sat up, and Persi and Neuro both jumped down. Alex stretched, adorable with his five o'clock shadow and sleepy expression. "I've been working overtime some while you were out of town."

"You work too hard."

He ran his fingers through his hair. "No such thing right now."

"Big case?"

"Every case is a big one when you're starting a practice."

"You're doing great. The whole town loves you." I offered a hand and helped him to his feet. "Look at Debbie."

He winced. "You could have talked all night and not said that."

"And here I was trying to help."

"I bet you were." He hugged me. "I've seen opposing attorneys more helpful than that."

"Well, fine then. If you want to slam my efforts to build up your self-esteem."

He kissed me on the forehead. "All kidding aside, you're the greatest." He jangled his keys. "Good night."

"Good night." I turned the dead bolt behind him.

"You know . . ." I said to Persi and Neuro. "It doesn't do any good to find Mr. Right if he doesn't have sense enough to know he's it."

I stood in the window and watched Alex's truck lights go down the driveway. The truth was, this wasn't about finding Mr. Right. Or even Mr. As-Good-As-It-Gets, as I'd joked to Carly a few years ago when I'd promised to try to find "the one" by my thirtieth birthday. I'd passed thirty a few months back, and the world didn't come crashing down around my ears. My reasonably happy-with-my-life card hadn't expired at the stroke of midnight. I had good friends, a wonderful family, and an amazing church congregation.

Unfortunately this was more personal than finding a husband. I'd committed dating's cardinal sin when I let myself fall in love with someone who might not feel the same way about me.

# 12

The simple inherit folly, but the prudent
are crowned with knowledge.

PROVERBS 14:18

The only good thing about working Saturdays was that Lisa wouldn't be caught dead here on a weekend. Mostly because of that, I'd been glad to volunteer to work today so I could be off Monday for the funeral. An hour after I opened, Bob walked into the office we shared.

"Jenna. Glad you finally made it back from vacation."

"Looks like y'all had a few problems while I was gone." I didn't mention the gossip about members walking out due to poor management.

"Yes. I told you Lisa wasn't ready for you to take a vacation. She tried her best, I'm sure. But she just wasn't ready." He shook his head, and I expected him to wipe a stray tear any minute.

*Well, you should have thought of that before you put her in my position.* I bit back the words. "Bob . . . I'm not sure she's ever going to be ready. She really hasn't learned much in the months she's been here."

"A student is only as good as her teacher."

I *know* he didn't just say that. "Are you implying that I don't know my job?"

"Oh, no. No, no. I didn't mean that. I just mean, if you'd been more patient with her . . ."

"Patient?" I counted to ten, and the last few numbers I didn't even try to hide what I was doing. "For months, I've been her built-in servant. She hasn't listened to me because you brought her in and let *her* tell *me* what to do."

"I told you, I wanted to help build up her self-esteem."

"By bossing me around?"

"Aw, now . . . she wasn't the boss."

"Well, she didn't get that memo, apparently."

He pointed at me. "You should have made it plain to her."

I pointed back, instinctively. "No, Bob, *you* should have made it plain to her. She's your daughter."

"You're right." He hung his head. "But

she's had it so rough lately. I just didn't want to hurt her any more." He looked so beaten down. "Wait until you have kids. It's not easy being a parent. Especially to a delicate girl like Lisa."

"I'm sure it's difficult. But you're going to explain it to her, right? That I'm the manager and she's an employee."

"Your assistant," Bob said, his expression switching from hangdog to bulldog in one fell swoop.

"Okay, my assistant." Even that would be an improvement since it had seemed like vice versa before.

"You mentioned taking more vacation time. Is that going to be soon?"

I nodded. "I have three more days, and that's just this year's vacation days. You know I haven't had a vacation since I started."

"I appreciate how dedicated you've been. But three more days is all I can spare you right now. We've got to get things back to normal around here."

With that parting shot, he walked out.

Normal? I glanced down at the nameplate on my desk. JENNA STAFFORD, MANAGER. Right beside it was Gail's list of irate members I needed to call. If I was going to spend all my time cleaning up someone else's mess, maybe I should change that title to Janitor.

Midafternoon, I was checking the chlorine level in the pool when Amelia strutted in. She slipped off her terrycloth robe and did a little pirouette as if to show me her white bikini.

"I wore white today, just in case." She nodded toward the pool. "Did you get it all straightened out?"

"Yes, the levels are fine. I'm so sorry that happened."

"Yes, well, me, too." She slid into the water and I slipped from the room. If the First Lady of Lake View was willing to forgive, maybe our other members would be, too. As Amelia goes, so goes Lake View might not be entirely accurate, but it was close.

Later that afternoon, I was washing my hands in the restroom when she came in, hair damp but fully dressed.

"So, Jenna, tell me. What was it like being around the great Holly Wood? Was she still as hard to get along with as she used to be?" Amelia carefully traced her lips with coral lip liner. "I know you aren't supposed to speak ill of the dead, but she was the most egotistical person I've ever known." The mayor's wife examined her face in the mirror.

"Really? I didn't realize you knew her that well." Way back in my more naive days, before I got to know Lisa or Holly, I had thought Amelia was self-centered.

"I didn't know her that well, but I did know Ruth."

"You were friends with Ruth?"

Amelia glanced at me.

"Let's just say she helped me get through some subjects that were too boring for me to spend time on."

If anyone else said that, I'd assume that Ruth tutored her. But with Amelia, I felt sure it meant Ruth did her work.

"Poor Ruth." Amelia filled in her lips with the coral lipstick.

"Poor Ruth?" I watched Amelia in the mirror. Maybe if I knew how to apply makeup like that, I wouldn't be wondering about Alex's feelings. On second thought . . . I'd rather be me. "Because her sister died?"

"Well that, too. But mostly because Holly was her sister." She dropped her lip liner and lipstick into her Prada handbag. "Ohh. I wonder if Ruth killed her." She raised a perfectly arched eyebrow at me. "You do know that Holly ran off with Ruth's husband, Cecil?"

"You're kidding. Her own sister? Now

that's cold." If I could have raised an eyebrow in return, I would have. I was surprised. But knowing Holly, I guess I shouldn't have been.

"I can't believe you didn't know that. Ruth and Cecil were married and had a little boy. Holly didn't keep Cecil long, though. He came crawling home with his tail between his legs and wanted Ruth to take him back."

"Did she? Where is he now?"

"I'm a little fuzzy on the details. After all, I *was* busy with my own life." She picked up her bag and gave me a little wave.

For some reason, the name Cecil seemed so familiar.

"Amelia!"

She stuck her head back in.

"If you figure out where Cecil is now, let me know, okay?"

She shook her finger at me. "Snooping again?" She grinned, her straight white teeth gleaming. "As long as I'm not your target, I'm happy to help."

Alex called mid-Proverb. I slid my bookmark between the pages and closed the Bible then flipped open my phone. "Hey."

"Hey, Jenna. How'd your day go?"

"Long." I'd come home at six and waited

an hour for Alex to call before I finally broke down and ate a single-serving microwave panini. After that, a long bubble bath, then bed and Proverbs.

"Were we going to do something tonight?"

I eyeballed the clock by my bed. "It's nine o'clock."

He sighed. "I'm sorry. I just finished working. Are you already tucked in for the night?"

All the way down to my Mickey Mouse nightgown. "Yep. Sorry. Mom invited us to eat with them after church tomorrow. How about that?"

Silence. "Actually, I need to go over some documents right after church. If I get hungry, I'll probably just grab a bite downtown and eat while I read."

"I understand." Sort of. Although the saying about all work and no play did jump into my mind.

"How about we get together Monday night after the funeral?"

"That sounds great, Alex. I'll see you then."

When we hung up, I turned back to Proverbs. I ignored my marked place and flipped over to chapter 31. All my life I'd heard people talk about being a virtuous Proverbs 31 woman. But it was hard. My eyes fell on verse 26. *"She speaks with wisdom. . . ."* I could sure use some wisdom, I thought sleepily.

I'm cleaning the tile around the pool with a toothbrush when Ruth and Cecil walk in. He actually looks just like Bob, but somehow I know he's Cecil.

"So you're the janitor here," Ruth says, tightening her grip on Cecil's arm. "You'll never get voted Most Virtuous Woman if you dress like that, you know."

I look down and gasp. Why am I wearing a white bikini? I stumble to my feet and grab a terrycloth robe from the stash of clean robes we keep for members only. With it wrapped tightly around me and cinched at the waist, I walk over to Ruth and Cecil. "Are y'all here for a swim?"

Suddenly the door opens and there stands Holly, looking vibrant in a blue evening gown. "I'm here for a manicure," she says, haughtily stepping toward us like she's walking down a runway.

Cecil drops Ruth's arm and runs to escort Holly to a poolside table. While Ruth and I look on, he sits down across from her, pulls out a manicure kit, and takes her hand in his. Wait, that's not Cecil. It *is* Bob. And the woman I thought was Holly is Bob's daughter, Lisa. The sparkling crown on her head should have been a dead giveaway.

I turn to explain the crown to Ruth. "She's Daddy's little princess, you know."

She nods. "She always was."

I frown. Is she talking about Lisa? Or Holly?

Before I can ask, Alex walks into the pool area, dressed for court and carrying his briefcase. "Hi," I call. "Want to go get something to eat?"

A frustrated look crosses his face. I see his lips move, but a sudden loud buzzing makes it impossible for me to hear what he's saying. Panicked, I look around for the source. The buzzing grows louder and I jump.

I sat up in bed, my heart pounding, and stared around my dimly lit bedroom. No Cecil, no Ruth, no Bob or Lisa. And especially no Alex. Just Neuro perched watchfully on my antique armchair and Mr. Persi snoring at the foot of the bed. And my alarm going off. Time to get up and get ready for church.

As soon as the closing prayer was over, Mama turned around in the pew in front of me. "You and Alex coming for dinner?"

I grimaced. "I am." Alex had come in late and sat in the back pew. I glanced around the building and didn't see him.

"Did y'all have a fight?" Mama looked concerned. "I warned you about going off on vacation and leaving him here."

"And I told you then, he's a grown man. Besides he came out to Branson, and we had a great time."

"Then why isn't he coming to dinner?"

"He has to work."

She clucked her tongue against the roof of her mouth in that age-old sign of shame. "I was just telling your daddy the other day, that boy works way too hard."

"That's not really our business," I said, hoping to gently remind her that Alex was not family. "I have to run by the house and let Mr. Persi out. See you in a few minutes."

"Hurry. The pot roast should be ready soon."

Well, that was some consolation. If I had to go solo to Sunday dinner, at least we were having my favorite.

Twenty minutes later, I parked around by the kitchen door at Mama's and hurried in. "That smells amazing."

Carly shoved a basket of rolls at me. "Put these on the table and we'll be ready to eat."

She picked up a pitcher of tea and led the way into the dining room.

Mama looked up from over by the buffet where she was putting ice in the glasses. "Your dad invited one of our cabin guests to eat with us."

Carly and I exchanged a look. Not that we had anything against hospitality, but all through the years, if a guest was alone and had interesting stories to tell, Daddy invited him or her for lunch. Sometimes it could get awkward.

The dining room door pushed open and the twins scurried to their seats, followed by Zac, who maintained his cool but hurried. Bringing up the rear was Daddy and . . .

I blinked my eyes. I *must* be seeing things.

"This is Detective Jim Jamison." Daddy introduced him to us all at one time. "I think you girls already know him."

Good thing I was already halfway into my chair. I think my knees gave way.

Jim nodded toward Carly and me.

"What are you doing here?" It just popped out even though I knew it was rude, especially when Mama gasped.

Mama threw me a look that plainly said she'd raised me with more manners than that. She motioned the detective to sit next to me then turned her attention back to her impolite daughter. "He's investigating Holly's murder."

Of course. I knew he hadn't followed me home. At least I was pretty sure of it.

After Daddy blessed the food, Jim looked at me. "I came in a little early to talk to some of Holly's childhood friends." He grinned. "And you've read enough murder mysteries to know the killer always goes to the funeral, right?"

I nodded, even though I knew he was making fun of me.

He smiled. "I can't take a chance on that being true and me not being here, can I?" He passed me the bread basket.

"I guess not." I buttered my roll, and for the next several minutes, I let the conversation swirl around me while I concentrated on pot roast, carrots, and potatoes.

"Fran LeMay told me Tom had to put off Joe Harrison's visitation and Sally Bearden's, too. They're going to use all the rooms tonight for Holly's."

As I bit into my roll, I thought about how Joe Harrison and Sally Bearden's families must have felt. The ninety-year-old baker and seventy-year-old wife and mother had been more a part of this community than Holly had. But fame demanded first place. Even in death.

I heard my name and looked up. "What?"

Daddy frowned. "I was just telling Jim that you'd probably be glad to show him the church building where the funeral is going to be before you head down to LeMay's for the visitation. And maybe take him over to the diner so he can meet some people."

That would teach me to pay more attention to what was going on. In my family the motto is, *you snooze, you get volunteered.* "Sure."

Carly coughed and I glared at her. If she wasn't careful, I'd volunteer her.

When we walked out the front door, Jim led me to a little silver sports car parked by the cabin closest to Mama and Daddy's house.

"This is your car?"

He jangled the keys and grinned. "What? Were you expecting a Crown Victoria?"

Heat flooded my face. Actually I *had* been looking for a policeman-type car. But I wasn't about to tell him that.

He held the door open for me, and I sank down into the low-slung car. Amazing how spoiled I was to an SUV. Luxury aside, I felt like I was going for a ride in a go-kart.

"Go up there to that big oak tree and take a right."

He looked over at me and raised an eyebrow. "What happens if the tree dies and falls down?"

I shrugged. "We'd say, 'Go up there to where that big oak tree used to be and take a right.' And in the meantime, we'd plant a new one."

"Of course you would. That makes perfect sense." He put on his right turn signal and made the turn. "In Lake View."

"You've only been in my hometown a few hours, and you're already making fun. That's not a good sign."

"I'm just kidding."

"Good. Go to the bottom of the hill and make a left."

"Why do you guys even name your streets?"

"It's just a formality."

"I can see that."

"The church building is on the right around the next curve."

He whipped the car into the parking lot and stopped in front of the old white clapboard building, its steeple almost as tall as the building was wide.

"Small," he murmured.

Was he talking about the building or his car? I'd seen lockers that looked roomier. Our faces were inches apart. Okay, maybe a couple of feet, but still . . . it was close quarters.

"The funeral is invitation only, plus a few press passes." Which of course he knew. Tell me again why he needed a tour guide? "So I guess Ruth figured it's big enough. It's where they attended as children."

"That makes sense."

I was tired of beating around the bush with men. Sometimes a little bluntness can go a long way. "Jim, why am I here?"

He stared at me for a few seconds, as if weighing his answer. "Because I thought it might give us a chance to get to know each other better. You'll be back in Branson, but only for a few days, then who knows if we'll ever see each other again?"

His eyes bored into mine. And just like always . . . read the truth.

"Which doesn't bother you a whole lot, right?" He gave me a self-deprecating grin. "I've been deluding myself, haven't I?"

My face burned, and I could only imagine how red it must look. "Jim, your ability to see straight to the marrow of the truth fascinates me. And I think you're a really nice guy. But . . ."

"I'm too old for you?"

If I'd been interested in him, fifteen years wouldn't have mattered. "Not really, but . . ."

"There's someone else."

"Yes. Maybe. At least for me — Oh, forget it." I ducked my head. "I'd love to be friends with you."

"Thinkin' it might be nice to have a detective consultant when you play Nancy Drew?"

"Have you been talking to our chief of police?"

"For quite a while this morning, now that you mention it. What was your first clue?"

We were still joking about John's opinion of my nosiness when we walked into the Lake View Diner and almost ran into Alex, who was holding a Styrofoam take-out container in one hand and his briefcase in the other.

Suddenly I remembered my dream. "Alex, this is Detective Jim Jamison. He came down from Branson for the visitation and funeral."

"Jim, this is my . . ." Now there was a stumper.

# 13

With his mouth the godless destroys his neighbor, but through knowledge the righteous escape.

PROVERBS 11:9

"This is my friend, Alex Campbell."

Jim offered his hand, and after a moment of hesitation that I may have completely imagined, Alex shifted his briefcase under his arm and accepted Jim's handshake. "Nice to meet you," he said softly and just stared at us, his brows drawn together.

Jim nodded. "You, too." He put his hand loosely on my forearm as if to guide me out around Alex.

"Good luck with your work," I said as I passed him.

He didn't answer. Did he think I was on a date with Jim? Was that why he looked so funny? I turned around to explain, but the door was already closing behind him.

For the next hour, I sat at the counter while Jim struck up conversations with locals. While I played with a straw, my bizarre dream drifted into my mind. Out of all the weirdness, the thing that puzzled me the most was why Cecil had been giving Holly a manicure.

As quickly as the question went through my mind, my breath caught in my throat. Cecil was CeeCee. That first night we met Holly, she'd been on the phone with Cee-Cee. Cecil. Of course. And she'd said that she'd see him Saturday. Yet no one mentioned Cecil being there. As far as I knew, the police hadn't questioned him. I looked over at Jim who was getting an earful from Debbie. I bet he didn't even know about Cecil.

I fidgeted until he finally came back over to me. "What are you dying to tell me?"

The words tumbled out as I told him about CeeCee and my discovery about Cecil. "Undoubtedly, he killed her."

"How many people have you thought were guilty since Holly's death?"

"What does that have to do with anything?"

"Just wondering if your muscles get sore from all that jumping to conclusions."

"So you aren't even curious about Cecil?"

He shrugged. "I'll look into it."

"So will I."

He shook his head. "Playing Nancy Drew is going to get you in serious trouble someday."

Photos of Holly flitted across the huge screen at the front of the viewing room. I stood toward the front, mesmerized by how normal her life appeared. Holly as a baby. Just like all babies, she was precious. Toddler Holly holding the hand of her older sister, looking up at her like she hung the moon. Holly at her sixth grade graduation, with her proud parents on either side of her. Then Holly on stage as a teenager, playing her guitar. And Holly beside Ruth, who cradled a baby in her arms.

A few slides later Holly and Ruth were each holding a hand of the young boy standing between them. With the next shot, Holly and Ruth by a Christmas tree while the same boy, only older and more sullen-looking, opened a huge wrapped box. That boy looked very familiar to me. I nudged Carly. "Is that Joey?"

She glanced around the room and lifted her hand in greeting to John and Marta who were talking to someone by the door. "Where?" she asked me distractedly.

"Never mind. He's gone now."

"Where did he go? What part of the room is he in?" Carly craned her neck.

I shook my head. "It was a picture. On the screen."

"Oh. I'll watch." Carly stood with her eyes glued to the screen until those snapshots came back around. "It sure looks like him."

"But if it is . . ."

"You said Holly ran off with his dad. That would explain the big Christmas present."

"Holly also ran off with Ruth's husband, Cecil, remember?"

"How could I forget —" Carly said a little sarcastically. "Cecil. Your numero uno suspect now."

"Do you also remember that Cecil left her *and* their little boy?"

Carly gasped. "Joey is Ruth's son."

"Nice detective skills, my dear Watson."

"So do you think he and his dad are in it together?"

I shrugged. "Stranger things have happened."

We walked over to Ruth. Thankfully, Carly led the way and stepped up to hug her. "I'm really sorry for your loss. Holly will be missed by so many people."

Ruth dabbed at her red-rimmed eyes with a handkerchief and looked out at the crowd behind Carly and me. "Yes. Everyone loved her."

*Well, obviously not everyone . . .*

Carly nudged me without even turning around.

I glared at her back. Making sure I said the right thing wasn't enough anymore. Now she was monitoring my *thoughts* in social situations.

I followed her lead, though, and hugged Ruth. "You chose beautiful pictures."

Her smile was teary. "Thanks. There were so many to choose from, but I wanted some that showed her private life as well as her public life."

Hard not to notice that none of them included Buck. But he'd have his day with the video montage he'd volunteered to have done for the memorial concert.

No sooner had the thought crossed my mind, than Ruth, glancing over our shoulders, stiffened. Fury played across her face. I knew without turning. But my curiosity wouldn't let me rest without seeing it for myself. I shifted toward the crowd and saw Buck coming straight toward us.

"That low-down hypocrite. How can he have the nerve to come up here and act all heartbroken when I know he's the one who killed my baby sister?" Ruth's voice rose on the last few words. Enough to draw the attention of the people nearest us.

Carly patted her on the arm, "Ruth, sugar, I know you're upset. This is a really hard day for you."

For a hopeful minute I thought it was going to work. Ruth seemed to relax just a little.

But Buck seemed unaware of the minefield he was about to enter.

"Ruth, we're going to miss her so much." He actually reached out like he was going to hug her.

Ruth jerked back and narrowed her eyes. "How dare you. Don't you even pretend that you cared about Holly. You murderer!" Every head in the room turned to look at the drama being played out in front of them. I saw Maurice making a beeline for her from the back of the room, but I knew he wouldn't be in time to stop the drama.

"Get a grip, Ruth. You know I didn't kill her." Buck dropped his hand. "Why would I? I loved her."

"You loved the lifestyle she kept you in." She glared at him. "And that five-million-dollar life insurance policy you had on her."

My ears perked up. Ruth had mentioned a life insurance policy before, but I never knew how big it was. Five million dollars was a pretty good motive for murder. I looked at Buck again and wondered how good an actor he was.

"She didn't even include me in her will." He sounded hurt that Holly had left him out.

"That's right. She didn't." Her voice dripped venom. "And no wonder with you running around with that floozy right under her nose." Ruth was doing the Dr. Jekyll thing again. From bereaved sister to attacking tiger.

I could practically feel all the cell phones with cameras pointing toward us.

"Can't you do something?" I hissed to Carly.

"Divide and conquer?" she whispered.

"Buck, come and let me show you some of the floral tributes to Holly." I reached out and took his arm to lead him away.

But apparently he wanted to have the last word, because he shrugged my hand away. "You have a lot of nerve acting all righteous. You were so jealous of her I wouldn't doubt if you killed her yourself."

Ruth's face whitened and she looked faint. "You mark my words, I'll see you behind bars before we're done." Maurice pulled her away and she sobbed on his shoulder.

I looked across the room where Chief

Detective Jim Jamison was watching and listening attentively. He lifted his chin at me and I nodded. Even Nancy Drew would have a hard time sorting out all the drama in this case.

Carly and I flashed the cards that Ruth had given us at the two security guards standing inside the foyer of the church building. We walked through the open double doors and I stopped. The smell of roses hung over the packed auditorium like an almost sickeningly sweet fog. An usher showed us to two seats halfway down the outside aisle. We kept our heads down, but a couple of times I glanced around to see if I recognized any stars. I didn't want it to look like Carly and I were paparazzi, or worse, stalkerazzi. Carly nudged me with her elbow as we sat down. "See that blond at the other end of our pew?" she whispered.

I leaned forward subtly then turned back to Carly. "Yeah?"

"Is that Carrie Underwood?"

I frowned. "No."

"Taylor Swift?"

I shook my head. "It's Rachel Jones."

Carly looked one more time and sat back. "What does she sing?"

"She's Mrs. Jones, the librarian's, granddaughter."

"Oh." Carly slouched down in the pew.

A familiar profile caught my eye. "But I do think that may be Brad Paisley four rows in front of us and toward the middle."

Carly squeezed my arm. "Really?"

Just then he turned all the way around to speak to a woman behind him and we both sighed. "That guy works at the post office," Carly said.

I nodded. "He sold me stamps yesterday."

The music started. I don't know what I'd expected, but maybe I'd thought that Ruth would have Holly's songs played. Instead a haunting tenor solo of "Amazing Grace" echoed through the room. Traditional hymns like "Beulah Land" and "Never Grow Old" followed.

Understandably, I expected a preacher to opine about Holly's passing, but when the last note of "Time Is Filled with Swift Transition" faded away, tradition ended abruptly. Maurice made his way up to the microphone and did a brief bio of Holly, presumably in case anyone had wandered into the wrong funeral. Then he asked for those who knew Holly well to feel free to say a few words about her.

He sat back down by Ruth as several people lined up for the microphone. An old man in creased khakis, a crisp blue shirt, and a fedora talked about being Holly's parents' neighbor since before she was born. He told stories of how when she was tiny everyone thought she would be the next Shirley Temple. And he reminisced about how proud her parents had been of her right up until their deaths.

Ruth sat at the front on the opposite side of the aisle from us. If I looked between the Brad Paisley look-alike and the woman behind him, I could see her profile. Best I could tell, she was stone-faced and dry-eyed.

Several people shared little tidbits of praise about Holly. Painted with the forgiving brush of death, Holly became perfect and untouchable. When Buck walked up to the microphone, I saw Ruth stiffen. Would she make another scene today? Or would grief and respect for her sister keep her quiet? From the look on her face, it was anybody's guess. I saw Maurice put his arm around her. Maybe so he could make her behave.

Buck stepped to the microphone, looking suitably mournful in his black suit and muted tie. He addressed the audience with a somber face, and to me it seemed clear he was purposely downplaying his natural exuberance. Or maybe it was just me. With the obvious exception of Ruth, everyone else seemed enthralled with him. "Holly was a wonderful person and a talented performer. She was the best wife a man could ever wish for." His voice quivered, but he got control. "She was warm, loving, and caring." The image of her screaming and throwing things at him in her dressing room jumped to the forefront of my mind. "I could never do enough for her, nor she for me. We were soul mates, and I'll cherish her memory forever." He paused to wipe his eyes.

"He might as well cherish it. I heard her memory is all he got," a gray-haired woman in front of us whispered loudly.

"Huh?" her equally gray companion said.

"She cut him out of the will."

Buck walked back to his seat as an embarrassed silence fell over the crowd.

Reagan, wearing a glittery little black number that looked like it belonged at the CMA awards instead of a funeral, carried her guitar up to the microphone. "Holly was my hero. She set the standard for every country music performer in America." Ruth started to stand, but Maurice pulled her back down. "With that in mind, I wrote a song especially for Holly that I'd like to sing in her honor."

Maurice, still with his arm tightly around Ruth's shoulder, whispered in her ear.

Reagan put her guitar around her neck and adjusted the mike. "For Holly," she said softly.

She strummed the opening notes, and with a teary smile, started to sing.

A deep voice across the aisle from us yelled, "Killer!"

My head whipped around. Where had that come from? I jumped up just as two loud explosions sounded in rapid succession. Carly screamed and tugged on my arm. "Get down."

A man stumbled into the aisle brandishing a gun.

# 14

The eyes of the LORD are everywhere,
keeping watch on the wicked
and the good.

PROVERBS 15:3

Chaos erupted. The woman beside us dove under the pew and pulled her husband down with her. The gray-haired couple huddled together. He put his arm around her and shielded her with his body.

The security guards converged on the shooter, but he waved his gun threateningly in their direction and they backed away. "She deserves to die!" he screamed. He ran out the back doors with the guards right behind him.

As soon as he was gone, I pulled Carly toward the front of the auditorium. Buck and a couple of security guards bent over Reagan, who lay on the floor like a bundle of rags — sparkly rags. Before we could get to her, John Conner, the Lake View chief of police, stepped in front of me. "Jenna, y'all please just sit back down."

I didn't move. "Did they catch him?"

"Is she dead?" Carly whispered.

"Sit down," John growled, but then he looked at Carly and gave an almost imperceptible shake of his head.

A security guard stepped to the microphone.

"Is there a doctor in the house? We need a doctor up here. Everyone else, sit down, please."

Carly and I eased back to our seats as several people answered the call for medical personnel. A teenager in a miniskirt stomped back to her seat, apparently furious that they had doubted her medical credentials.

For a few seconds, the clicking of cell phone cameras was all that could be heard. Then Tom LeMay, the funeral director, walked up and stood next to the rose-draped casket. His face and even his bald head were almost as red as the roses.

"If he doesn't loosen his tie, we're going to have another casualty," I whispered to Carly, and she nodded.

"Ladies and gentlemen," Tom began, slightly stammering. "Please remain calm."

He pulled a white handkerchief from his pocket and wiped his face. "The . . . um, assailant has been apprehended." In the distance, the whine of an ambulance siren grew louder. "We're going to clear the building in an orderly manner to allow the EMTs room to work." He nodded toward his suit-clad assistant, who stood by the back row directing people outside. "Please get in your vehicles, and we'll continue to the burial at Eight Mile Cemetery as planned."

In that unique way that funeral directors have, he had the auditorium cleared within five minutes.

Outside, I blinked against the sunshine, unaccountably cheery and bright. "Do you think John was saying that Reagan's alive?" Carly asked.

I motioned toward Marta, who was standing near her vehicle in the lineup to go to the cemetery. "Maybe Marta knows."

We started across to her but stopped as an ambulance squealed into the parking lot. Two EMTs jumped out and ran into the building.

"At least they're in a hurry," I said.

Carly nodded. "Always a good sign."

When we reached Marta, she hugged us both. "I'm so glad y'all are here. Do you think one of you could go with Reagan to the hospital?"

"I will," I said.

"Is she alive?" Carly asked.

"She was earlier. I'm praying she still is."

I nodded. "So are we. Do you know how to get in touch with her family?"

"From what she told me, she was a foster child."

"Bless her heart." Carly wiped her eyes.

Marta's eyes filled with tears, too. "Yeah. She's twenty-two."

I thought about the sometimes pouty, sometimes sultry singer. "Just a kid, really."

Carly shook her head. "And no mama or daddy."

"I know it." Marta looked toward Ruth and Maurice sitting in the limo behind the hearse. "I hate not to follow the ambulance, but I don't want to leave Ruth."

My heart went out to Marta. She was going to be the perfect innkeeper. With all her guests' foibles and faults and even knowing there might be a murderer among them, she'd taken them under her wing like a mother hen with her chicks.

"Did she come with you?" Carly asked.

"No, Reagan did." Marta looked worriedly toward the building. "Ruth rode with Maurice." She motioned toward a low-slung red car in the parking lot. "But Ruth was complaining about not having any leg room. She might want to ride home with me, now that Reagan . . ."

I touched her arm. "Don't worry about the hospital. I'll be there if Reagan needs anything."

She hugged me again. "Thanks. Carly, will you ride with me to the cemetery?"

"Unless you want me to go with you, Jenna?"

"No, you go on and help Marta with Ruth. I'll probably spend all my time sitting in a waiting room anyway."

As white-faced as Marta already was, I hated to bring it up, but I needed to know. "So did you hear anything about the shooter? Who it might be?"

She stared at me. "Didn't y'all see him?"

"Only for a second from the back. Was it someone we know?"

"You could say that," Marta said. "It was the stalker."

Of course it was. As I remembered the things he yelled, I wondered why I didn't realize that immediately.

The Lake View Hospital ER was packed when I walked in. I smiled at the receptionist. "My . . ." I paused. What was Reagan to me? I'd come mostly out of pity and out of a desire to help Marta. "Reagan Curtis was brought in earlier. A gunshot wound? Where is she now?"

The harried woman glanced up at me. "What's your relationship to Ms. Curtis?"

"I'm as close to family as she has nearby." Unless you counted the man she was having an affair with when his wife was killed. But in terms of giving information, sometimes less is more.

She shoved a clipboard of forms toward me. "Fill these out, please." She turned away from me.

"In order for you to tell me where she is?" I knew paperwork had almost taken over the medical world, but this was ridiculous.

A puzzled expression crossed her plump face. "We have to have these filled out, and you said you were her next of kin."

"I'll answer what I can. And what I can't, maybe I can get the answers for you. Okay?"

"Okay." Her tone indicated that she thought I was one page short of a complete document.

"I'll take these with me and fill them in. But right now, I need to know where Reagan is and how she's doing." First rule of negotiation. Get something for each concession you make.

She considered my offer for a few tense

seconds then gave in with a sigh. "She's in surgery right now. After that, they'll move her to the ICU. You can wait in the ICU waiting room, and the surgeon will come out and see you when they're finished."

She quickly gave me directions. "Bring those forms back to me when you get them done," she called as I bolted down the hall.

I waved at her over my shoulder.

In the ICU waiting room, I glanced at the huddled groups of people and sat on a padded chair away from the others. I smoothed down my black skirt. I should have gone by the house and changed, but I'd been in too big a hurry to check on Reagan. I turned my attention to the clipboard. Name. Got that covered. Birth date. Uh-oh. This farce had gotten me into the waiting room, but if I went back up and told the receptionist that I didn't know Reagan's birthday or her address, would the surgeon still keep me posted on her condition? Somehow I doubted it.

I called Marta.

She answered on the first ring. "Jenna? How's Reagan?"

I groaned quietly. "I don't know. And I'm not likely to find out if you don't help me."

"What do you need?"

"Who has Reagan's purse?"

"I do. Why?"

I explained the information I needed, and within minutes, the three of us — Marta, Reagan's purse, and I — had the forms completed.

"Carly's here. She said she'd bring Reagan's insurance card by in a while."

I quickly took the paperwork back to the receptionist then rushed back to the ICU waiting room. And waited.

After a seemingly interminable time, a man in surgical scrubs appeared at the door. "Is anyone here with Ms. Curtis?"

I followed him to a small room where he gestured to a chair. I dropped into it. He sat across from me. "One bullet grazed Ms. Curtis's skull. Thankfully it didn't penetrate. The other one lodged in her thigh. We removed it, and I think we have the blood loss under control."

I nodded, processing the fact that Reagan was alive. A little of the tension drained away.

He continued, "In about an hour, you'll be able to see her for a few minutes. A nurse will let you know when you can go in. Ms. Curtis will be in ICU at least overnight."

I thanked him. On my way back to the waiting room, my phone vibrated in my little black purse. I fished it out. "Hello?"

"Jenna. Are you okay?"

We were supposed to go out after the funeral. I'd completely forgotten. "Oh, Alex. About our date —"

"Jenna, I'm not worried about that." He almost sounded irritated with me. "I heard about the shooting. Are you okay? Where are you?"

I told him about Reagan.

"I'll be right there."

"As much as I'd love to see you . . ." As I said the words, I was overwhelmed with a longing to feel his strong, safe arms around me. But there was nothing he could do here. "I wish you could go by and let Mr. Persi out and check on Neuro instead."

Silence.

"Alex?"

"Sure. I'll go check on the animals. So you don't want me to come out there?" There was something indefinable in his voice.

"I guess not. I should get to see Reagan in a little while. Then I'm not sure what I'll do."

"You sound tired."

"I am. Today's been pretty stressful."

"I know it has." His tone softened. "I want to hear all about it. About that date . . . Can we reschedule for tomorrow night?"

As much as I wanted to see Alex right that second, I felt like I could sleep forever. And I knew how busy he was. "Why don't we just get through the workweek and make it Friday night?"

Silence again.

Was he upset that I'd been at the diner with Jim? I considered explaining. But why should I, really?

He cleared his throat. "Friday night's fine."

"We can just go to the diner then get a video after or something," I said, anxious to take the pressure off him.

"Actually, I —" he started.

A nurse stuck her head in the waiting room door. "Is anyone here with Reagan Curtis?"

"Alex, I've got to go. They're going to let me see Reagan now. Thanks for taking care of things at my house."

"You're welcome."

" 'Bye." I flipped the phone shut as I followed the nurse out into the hall. We almost bumped into Carly, who was coming in.

"Hey, you're just in time. We're going to go see Reagan."

Carly held up a little bag. "Let me leave this in the waiting room and I'll be right there."

I nodded and almost ran to catch up with the nurse. "Is she awake?" I asked.

She shrugged. "That's a matter of opinion. She's still really drowsy. So she may not remember much about this visit."

"Maybe that will keep her from wondering why you and I are the ones visiting her," Carly murmured in my ear.

I jumped and shushed her. The nurse looked back at us and frowned, but she pushed the round silver button on the wall and directed us into Reagan's cubicle.

I bit back a gasp. Carly put her hand over her mouth, her eyes wide. Reagan had bandages around the top of her head. Her face white, her eyes closed, she looked like she belonged in a morgue instead of a hospital. Except for the tubes everywhere. How could this be the same woman who'd looked so vibrant this afternoon?

Carly reached out and gently touched her arm. Reagan's eyes fluttered open and she moaned. Carly started to move her hand away, but Reagan grabbed it. "Don't leave." Her confused gaze darted from Carly to me. "I'm scared."

"We're here," I murmured. "Do you want us to pray for you?"

"Please," she whispered. She moaned again then drifted back to sleep. Or out of consciousness. I wasn't sure which.

We stood over her bed and prayed. Then we stayed, without talking, until the nurse gave us the signal to leave.

Out in the hall, Carly glanced at me. "Is she going to be okay?"

I told her what the surgeon had said. We went into the ICU waiting room, and Carly nodded toward the bag. "I brought some extra clothes in case you had to wait longer to see her than you thought you would."

"You're a lifesaver."

She shrugged. "A little late, though. You can just go home to change now."

"I'm not leaving."

She smiled at me. "You're way more tenderhearted than you let on, you know it?"

"How do you know I'm not just staying to see what I can learn?"

"Because I saw your eyes when we were in there with that girl. You were thinking about how awful it would be not to have any family to stay with you."

"And thankfully you feel that way, too." I picked at an imaginary piece of lint on my skirt then raised my gaze to hers. "Because I have to go to work tomorrow."

She laughed softly. "If you want to stay tonight, I'll take over in the morning in time for you to get home and get ready for work."

"Thanks, Car. That would be perfect."

"Now go change and I'll wait so we can visit at least until time to go see her again."

She didn't have to tell me twice. I slipped into the restroom and changed into the sweatpants and sweatshirt from the bag Carly had packed. I was so glad she'd taken into account the cool year-round temperature of hospital waiting rooms.

Dressed and comfortable finally, I plopped down beside Carly. "Thanks again."

"You're welcome. So I don't guess you've heard any news, huh?"

I looked around the deserted waiting room. "The rumor mill is very close-mouthed around here. Do you know anything?"

"Apparently the stalker pretty much surrendered in the church parking lot." She pulled her leg up under her and got comfortable. "Oh! And get this. Guess how he got in?"

"By invitation?"

"Nice guess, wise girl, but he used a press pass to get by the guards."

"Stolen?"

Carly ran her hands through her hair and fluffed out her curls. "No! Apparently he's a reporter for one of the lesser-known country music fan mags. So he had a legitimate pass."

"No wonder Holly was so nice to him. My guess is she's dominated that particular magazine's content for the last few years."

"Exactly."

"But talk about stalkerazzi. Sounds like he invented the term." One thing was still bothering me. "Why did he shoot Reagan?"

"Seems his mag had gotten a 'scoop' about Reagan and Buck having an affair. In the end, he said he thought the two of them had killed Holly."

"Wonder if John and Detective Jamison believe him?"

She shrugged. "He's been arrested for shooting Reagan. So far that's all I know about that."

"Do you think Reagan killed Holly?"

Carly frowned. "No."

"Why not?" I tended to feel the same way, but I needed someone to verbalize reasons.

"She's so young." She looked up at me, and I know she could see I was about to start naming all the young killers in history. She sighed. "I just don't think she did. She's childish and flighty and didn't use the best moral judgment, but I don't think she's a murderer."

"I agree. Plus she wouldn't have used a

guitar string. And anyway, I think she really did hero-worship Holly, and it just seems unnatural to kill your hero. But if she didn't, who did?"

"Buck?" Carly offered.

"He had motive," I said thoughtfully. "Even though he signed an airtight prenup agreement, remember what Ruth said at the funeral home — he had that huge life insurance policy on Holly."

Carly rummaged in her purse and pulled out a pen and a Wal-Mart receipt. She flipped the receipt over and wrote, *Buck — life insurance.* Then she looked at me. "And even though he was coming from the opposite direction, he could have easily killed Holly then doubled back."

She scrawled the word "Opportunity" beside his name and motive.

"You're right. And don't forget Cecil."

Carly frowned. "I know I teased you about making a man we've never seen your main suspect. But what *do* we really know about Cecil?"

"We know Holly was talking to him the night we walked in on her. And she told him she'd see him Saturday."

"But no one saw him Saturday."

"Maybe because he slipped in and killed

her then slipped back out. Never to be seen again."

She wrote, *Cecil — the Phantom Killer* on the receipt.

It did sound a little silly when she put it like that.

Pen poised, she twisted her lips. "Motive?"

I shrugged. "Who knows? Leave that blank for now." I pointed at her list. "You need to go ahead and add Reagan. We can't eliminate people based on gut instinct."

She put Reagan's name under Cecil's. "Motive?"

"Jealousy?"

She jotted it down. "She had the opportunity, I guess, during that ten minutes before she had to come back out and sing again."

"I wonder where she ranks on Detective Jamison's suspect list."

Carly held up the scribbled-on receipt. "Think he'd do a temporary trade so we could see?"

I laughed. "Somehow I doubt it."

The ICU waiting room door swished open.

Buck, his black suit rumpled and his face drawn, stepped into the room.

# 15

Hatred stirs up dissension, but love
covers over all wrongs.

PROVERBS 10:12

Carly's face paled, and she stuffed the
receipt into her purse.

He nodded to us. "Am I interrupting?"

"No, not at all." Carly's voice was nervous.
I looked at her. Was she thinking the killer
had come to finish us off for suspecting him?

"Have you seen her?"

"Yes." What was he doing here? Even in
the best of times, his presence was in bad
taste.

"How is she?"

"They think she's going to be okay." I
thought about her bandaged head and
tubes. And especially her pale face. "She
looks pretty bad, though."

He flinched. "It's all my fault." Without
being asked, he slipped into the seat directly

across from us and put his head in his hands.

Carly and I looked at each other. Then she cleared her throat. "You didn't cause her to get shot . . . did you?"

He raised his head, and for a minute, I thought he'd forgotten we were even there. "I should have left her alone from the beginning. She was just a kid who wanted to be a star. And I took advantage of that."

If he was about to tell us the intimate details of his relationship with Reagan, I'd rather not know.

"Holly was different than any woman I ever knew." He met our gaze and his eyes were hollow. "She was like a rare butterfly that would fly into your world briefly" — he reached out his hand and closed it on thin air — "but could never be held on to for long."

I wasn't sure how we'd jumped from Reagan over to Holly, but he obviously needed to talk, so Carly and I both just nodded.

"I fascinated her. Especially as long as I played the field. She was so used to total adoration that a little challenge went a long way."

I bit back a snort. "So you cheated on her to keep her from leaving you."

He sat back in the chair and nodded like

I'd answered the final *Jeopardy!* question. "Exactly."

Twisted and crazy, but I could see his logic. "And Reagan was available."

Sadness flitted across his face again. "Yeah. She was."

"So after Holly's death, you two could be together, right?" Carly's brows were drawn together.

He frowned. "What was the point after Holly was gone?"

"So you both were just trying to get Holly's attention?" she said thoughtfully.

"I guess you could say it like that."

No one spoke for a minute, and he stared absently over our heads at the muted TV up in the corner.

"Why do you feel responsible for Reagan getting shot?" I didn't want to leave this awkward conversation without finding that out, at least.

Still looking at the television, he answered slowly. "Even though I knew it would be tacky, I went along with her bringing her guitar to the funeral and singing that song she wrote for Holly."

"Why?"

He brought his gaze back down to me. "She said I owed it to her. To help her make atonement. And I decided she was right."

236

Were we about to hear a confession? Suddenly the waiting room seemed very deserted. "Atonement? For what?"

Carly nudged me with her elbow. I knew she was thinking I should quit asking questions.

"Not for killing her, if that's what you're thinking. Even the police know neither one of us did it." He squirmed in his seat. "Well, at least they know Reagan didn't. I guess they think I could have before I went to meet her."

"You went to meet her?"

"The night Holly was killed, Reagan sent me a note asking me to meet her in her dressing room after her set. So I did. She told me that she hated what we were doing. And that she wanted to stop. I tried to talk her out of it. But she wouldn't have it any other way."

"We were still there arguing when the stagehand came to tell us that Holly hadn't shown up and Reagan needed to go back out to stall."

"So she went back out, and you went looking for Holly."

"And ran into you in the hall."

Mentally I drew a big black line through Reagan's name on our suspect list and a thinner, more tentative one through Buck's.

He rubbed his hand over his face. "I never should have let her sing. Then that crazy stalker wouldn't have shot her."

"She's going to be okay," Carly said.

I nodded, pity overriding my extreme distaste. "Visiting time is in thirty minutes if you want to go in and see for yourself."

He shook his head and pushed to his feet. "I'm heading back to Nashville. Hopefully Reagan can forget she ever knew me."

"Will you be at the tribute concert for Holly a week from Friday?"

He nodded. "I wouldn't miss it." He opened the door then turned back. "I know it's hard for people like you to understand. But I did love her."

People like us? I guess he meant people who didn't live in a world where a man cheated on his wife in order to keep her.

The door swished shut behind him, and Carly slumped in her seat. "For a minute, I thought we were going to hear a murder confession."

"Me, too."

She slapped me on the arm. "Don't sound so disappointed. The reason murderers are talkative is because they're going to kill the person — or should I say people — they're spilling their guts to."

I rubbed my arm. "So get your list out."

She fished it from her purse and read over it. "If we believe Buck, then that just leaves Cecil."

"That's just because we're not done yet. Don't forget Joey. And Ruth."

"And the personal assistant Holly fired," Carly drawled.

"Oh, you're right. We could call her about the tribute preparations and maybe figure out if she was mad enough to kill over losing her job."

Carly grunted. "We filled in as Holly's personal assistants for a few days. Would you have been mad about losing that job? That woman probably drove home singing, 'Hallelujah' at the top of her lungs."

I smiled at the image. "Good point. Leave her off the list for now."

Carly and I hashed out suspects and motives for a while then she put the list back into her purse. "So did Mama tell you that Harvey and Alice are probably going to sell the diner?"

I nodded. "She's all worried about it. Afraid that their guests won't have anywhere to eat. But there are other places. Besides, maybe whoever buys it will be a great cook."

"Yeah." She fiddled with her hair. "Maybe."

"Carly? What's going on?"

"I don't know. Since I found out they wanted to sell, I can't quit thinking . . ."

"Oh! You're thinking about buying it?"

"No!" She ducked her head. "Yes. Maybe."

"Glad to see you've made up your mind."

She blushed. "It's crazy for me to even think about it. Imagine me, running the diner."

"Pretty easy to imagine, actually. I think you'd be a natural."

"Thanks, Jenna. Even though it'll probably never be more than a dream, it's fun to talk about it." She pointed to the clock on the wall. "It's almost nine. Time to go see Reagan. Then I have to get home."

Reagan, sound asleep, looked marginally stronger, but she still didn't appear to be out of the woods.

"She's been crying," Carly whispered and pointed to the moisture glistening on her cheeks beneath the plastic tubing.

I nodded and covered Reagan's hand with mine. Who wouldn't cry?

She shivered.

I pulled the blanket up over her shoulders and looked across the bed at Carly, who had her head bowed and her eyes closed. I joined her in a silent prayer for this young woman who right now looked more like a lost little girl.

Sleeping — or trying to — on waiting room chairs tended to make the next day seem long. And Tuesday didn't need much help to seem like the longest workday ever. By the end of the day, my muscles ached and my head hurt, but at least Lisa's lack of supervision at the athletic club was no longer so evident. Except in my office, I noted sourly, glaring at the art deco prints she'd hung in place of the beach scene prints Bob and I had agreed on when we first started sharing this office. I'd run across my pictures behind a shelf in the pool supply closet when I'd gone to check on a filter. Along with various other items Lisa had apparently stuffed out of the way. Such as pool maintenance schedules.

Like Mama always said, least said, soonest mended, so I'd kept my mouth shut. Now as I stretched and strained to get the pictures exactly back where they had been, I was thinking it might be worth a little mending to rip something.

Lisa had steered clear of me so far today, which was all good. Club members were getting back on their normal schedules, and most complaints had been cleared up. I was still doing all the work Lisa was supposed to do, but it was such a relief to have things running smoothly, I could live with that. As long as I didn't have her underfoot.

"Jenna." I heard her voice calling from down the hall, but before I could reply she opened the door and walked into my office without so much as a knock. "Oh. Here you are. I've looked everywhere for you."

I gritted my teeth. "Here I am. In my office." I adjusted the last picture and turned to face her. "What do you need?"

"One of the customers wanted an 'Get in the Swim with Jenna Stafford' T-shirt in blue. All I can find are pink ones. Where are the blue ones?"

She sounded so disgusted with the thought of my name being on a T-shirt that I smiled. "We only have pink ones." Bob had insisted on pink ones for a reason that only he knows. I begged for another color, especially considering my hair is red, and pretty-in-pink for redheads is really just a movie gimmick. But no, he'd insisted on pink and pink only. I didn't have to wear them, he'd said. Just sell them.

"Well, that's not very smart, is it? Why didn't you order blue ones? Not everyone likes pink."

Deep breath. "I didn't order the shirts. Your dad did. And I don't know why he chose pink. Why don't you ask him?"

"Well, you don't have to get huffy about it." Lisa shot me a venomous look. "Place a new order."

She snapped her fingers at me. I blinked. Did she really just do that? I was going to hyperventilate from all the deep breaths I needed if she didn't get out. "Lisa, I don't order shirts. That's Bob's department. You need to talk to him if you're not happy with the selection."

"I don't need to talk to Dad about anything. You work for us. Now order blue shirts." Lisa turned on her heel and walked out without a backward glance.

After she was gone, I paced. It really had been a long day. And if I did something hasty like quit on the spot, I'd probably regret it. Possibly. Maybe Carly would let me waitress at her imaginary diner. I envisioned myself taking orders and balancing five plates on my arm. That would be good, honest work, and I might not be half bad at it. But what would happen when I started wanting to sprint from table to table and do calisthenics in between orders?

Poor Carly. I could just see her having to install a pool in the dining area to keep me happy. Might not be bad for business, but I don't think she'd like it.

Instead, I'd just thank God that the workday only had another few minutes of life left in it and get things ready to close. As I went through my checklist — a list, I might add, that remained untouched while Lisa was in charge — I thought about how mad she'd be when she found out I didn't order the shirts.

"Tomorrow is another day," I muttered to the empty office. "Just call me Scarlett."

Right now what I wanted was a good book and a long bubble bath. *And a slightly less active conscience,* I thought wryly, as it reminded me that I needed to get back to the hospital. I'd checked with Carly a few minutes ago, and they were getting ready to move Reagan into a regular room. So I'd have to settle for saying "hi" and "good-bye" to my animals and taking a quick shower.

Carly met me in the main lobby. "They should have her in a room up on the second floor when you get up there."

"Good. How is she?"

She shrugged. "She's slept most of the day. The last time I went in to see her, she was a little more alert."

"That's good."

"I'm glad you think so, because she asked

me about who shot her."

"What did you say?"

"The nurse came in right then to ask me to leave so they could get her ready to move. So I said you'd tell her all about it when you got here."

I laughed. "You did not . . ." My voice trailed off as I noted Carly's abashed grin. "You did! You dumped that on me?"

"I sure did. And don't act like you wouldn't have done the same, sugar. I was afraid I'd say the wrong thing."

"What about me saying the wrong thing?"

"Well, this way you've got time to think it over."

"True." I gave her a hug and waved. "I'll take the stairs and think while I walk."

"If you don't want to tell her, just turn on the news. I'm sure it's all over the television," she called back over her shoulder.

"Thanks for the tip," I muttered and headed up the stairs.

I beat Reagan to the room, but within seconds they wheeled her in, bed and all. She gave me a weak smile while the nurse checked her vital signs and filled out her chart. I waved but stayed quietly in the corner until the nurse and attendant had both gone. "How're you feeling?" I asked.

"Like somebody shot me."

"Ouch." I stood and moved to a chair closer to the bed.

She started to nod but stopped and raised her hand to touch the bandage on her forehead. "Who did this?"

I didn't answer immediately.

"Who shot me?" she clarified.

"Did you know Holly had a stalker?"

"Yes. Buck —" She stopped. "I heard she did."

"Well, apparently her stalker came to the funeral and shot you."

Her brows drew together. "Why?"

What could I say? Maybe it would have been easier to just turn on the TV and let the anchorwoman tell her. "He's a freelance writer for a fan mag, and he heard you and Buck were having an affair."

She flinched. "So why shoot me now? Holly is dead."

Might as well get all the tough questions over with. "He claims that you killed Holly."

I didn't think it was possible, but her face grew whiter. "I didn't."

I covered her cold hand with mine. "I know. Buck told me you two were together."

"I was breaking it off with him."

I nodded. "He told me."

She raised her hand to her forehead and covered her eyes with her fingers. "You must think I'm an idiot."

"I think we all do stupid things some-times."

She peeked at me between her fingers, and a ghost of a smile flitted across her pale face. "You're tactful."

I grimaced. "Compared to my mama and my sister, I stomp in like an elephant in a dollhouse."

She started to laugh then groaned. "Hurts my head to laugh."

"Oh, I'm sorry."

"Don't be." She nodded toward the TV up in the corner. "Do you think we could watch the news?"

I hesitated, trying to exercise the tact she thought I had.

"Don't worry. I know what kinds of things they'll be saying about me."

"We can turn it off if you change your mind." I clutched the remote clipped to the bedsheet and hit the POWER button then switched the channel to an entertainment news station.

After a little of the latest celebrity gossip, a split screen of Holly and Reagan popped up behind the blond anchorwoman. "In breaking news, freelance writer, Rick Clarkson, who was charged earlier with the shooting of singer Reagan Curtis has now been charged with the murder of beloved queen of country music, Holly Wood."

I gasped. "No way."

The blond finished, "We'll bring you live updates of this case as we get them."

Reagan glanced over at me. "You don't think he did it?"

"No. And I can't imagine why they do."

She pursed her lips in a pout. "Because he said I killed her?"

I shook my head. "It's complicated. Maybe he did do it. But I just didn't think so." I slipped my cell phone wallet from my purse. "Would you excuse me for a minute? I need to step out and make a phone call."

"Sure." But her voice was tinged with worry.

"I'll be right back," I assured her.

"No problem."

Out in the hall, I fished out Detective Jamison's card and punched in his cell phone number on it.

"Detective Jamison here," he growled.

"Jim? It's Jenna Stafford."

"Jenna? How are you?"

"I'm fine. But you didn't seriously charge the stalker with Holly's murder, did you?"

For a second, I thought the cell phone had dropped the call. But finally he spoke. "Yes, we did. Do you have a problem with that?"

I lowered my voice. "Is this some kind of trap for the killer?"

"No," he whispered. "We have the killer."

# 16

A simple man believes anything, but a
prudent man gives thought to his steps.
PROVERBS 14:15

"What kind of proof do you have that he murdered Holly?"

"Not that I'm required to share my proof with you, but we matched those unknown prints at the murder scene to his."

I slapped my forehead with my hand. "Of course you did. He told us that Holly let him in Saturday morning, remember?"

"Well, that's his story. But even when you told me about him saying that, I wondered if he'd been in there Saturday night instead."

"Did he confess?"

"I'm not at liberty to discuss this any further with you, Jenna."

"Fine. Some tabloid will have all the details by tomorrow anyway."

He chuckled. "Be that as it may, those details won't have come from me. Oh, by the way. One consolation for you being wrong. With the killer behind bars, your friends' upcoming tribute concert will be a huge hit."

" 'Bye."

"See you in Branson." His cheery voice got on my last nerve.

Back in Reagan's room, she was talking on the house phone. When I walked in, she said, "I've got company. I'll talk to you later," and hung up.

"Hey."

"What did you find out?"

I hit MUTE on the remote control. "What do you mean?"

"On the phone. You went out to get your own scoop on the shooter being charged with Holly's murder, didn't you?"

This girl was far from an idiot.

"Something like that. I didn't find out much. They really did charge him."

"But you still don't believe he did it."

I shrugged. "If the police think he's guilty, who am I to argue?"

She considered my words for a moment then gave me a feeble smile. "I'm glad they think so. I hope they're right."

"Why?"

She nodded toward the house phone. "That was Joey, calling to check on me."

"Oh?" I hadn't pictured Joey as the solicitous type.

She bit her bottom lip. "You know it was his string."

"His string?"

"His guitar string."

"Guitar? Oh, *the* guitar string." Around Holly's neck, of course. "How do you know that?"

"All I know is he and I use the same kind of guitar strings. According to the cops, that's the brand that was used to kill Holly."

"So if it wasn't yours . . ."

"Exactly. It must have been his. Besides, he broke a string that night and went backstage to get another one."

"Did you tell the police?"

She stared over my shoulder at the window. For a minute, she didn't answer. Finally she met my gaze. "I didn't want to. But I had to. Because what if he did it?"

"You had no choice," I agreed.

A tear slid down her cheek. "I'm so glad they decided it wasn't him."

"Yeah." I didn't say any more, but my mind raced. What if Joey had killed Holly? Had the good detective been so eager to wrap up this case that he'd charged the wrong man with the crime? I couldn't help but wonder.

Dear Pru,
   I love my job, but I dread going to work because of one coworker. She's an obnoxious, bossy know-it-all, and I can barely stand to be in the same room with her. I know I'm not the only person who feels this way because I've heard others talking about her. Should I quit my job?
                                   In a Dilemma

Dear In a Dilemma,
   Minimize direct contact with this person as much as possible and still do your job. Make use of e-mails, voice mails, and even sticky notes if you must. Hang in there and bite your tongue. Coworkers come and coworkers go. Jobs you love aren't easy to come by.

Midafternoon Friday, Mama called me at the athletic club.

"I just have to know." Her voice was so quiet I could barely hear her.

"Mama?" After an exhausting week of working during the day and visiting Reagan at night, I wasn't up to a guessing game. "Know what?"

"Did you write that Ear-Day U-Pray letter?" she whispered.

"What are you talking about?" My pig Latin wasn't so rusty that I didn't recognize the words *Dear Pru.* But how could Mama possibly know I was Dear Pru? Carly was my only confidante, and we'd both been really careful.

She sighed. "I just got the paper. And I always read Dear Pru first, of course. Especially in the last year or so, it's gotten to be really good."

Her praise rendered me speechless. I finally opened my mouth to thank her and confess, just as she hissed, "So tell me the truth. I won't breathe a word. Are you in a dilemma?"

"Well, maybe a little." What kind of question was that? I'd promised never to tell anyone but Carly that I was Dear Pru, so with Mama asking me straight out, that definitely put me in a bit of a dilemma.

"What do you mean, a little? Did you write the letter about not liking your co-worker or not?"

Ohh. "No!"

"Are you sure?"

"Yes, I'm sure."

I could hear the paper rattling in the background. "Well, then you need to read this. Dear Pru gave In a Dilemma some wonderful advice that you'd do well to take to heart."

"Jenna!" Lisa yelled down the hallway.

I rolled my eyes. "I will, Mama. I promise. I get off work in five minutes, so I need to go get ready." And see if I could make Lisa see the wisdom of Dear Pru's advice. An e-mail yell would be much easier to take. Surely.

She burst into my office. "Some big shot is parked out on the curb. You need to go tell them we're closed."

I walked over to the window. A sleek black limo with dark windows was pulled up to the sidewalk in front of the club entrance. I glanced at her. "No one has gotten out of it?"

"No."

"Is Amelia here? Or Byron? Maybe this is a new perk for Lake View's first family. Being picked up from the health club by a limo."

Lisa tossed her brunette hair over her shoulder and crossed her arms in front of her. "Hmph. In this hick town? I don't think so. Anyway, no one's here. It's closing time."

"Fine. I'll grab my things and handle it on my way out." Gail — supposedly with Lisa's help — was doing the actual closing routine since I had a date tonight. Assuming Alex remembered to show up. We'd barely talked all week.

She watched me as I dropped my cell phone into my purse, put the strap on my shoulder, and grabbed my keys. I wanted to make a smart remark about her taking inventory or being sure I didn't steal anything, but I took my favorite advice columnist's advice and kept my mouth shut.

As I walked down the sidewalk toward the limo, my curiosity almost made me run. Had some of Holly's Nashville friends stayed in town after the funeral? For three days? I mentally scoffed at myself.

The limo driver had a chauffeur's uniform on including the hat. He stared straight ahead as I approached his window. But when I tapped on the glass, he rolled it down immediately.

"Sir, I'm sorry, but we're closing." I craned my neck to see who was in the back of the car, but the partition was up.

"Yes, ma'am. I know. Are you Jenna Stafford?"

I jerked my attention back to him with a snap. "Yes." As soon as I said yes, I realized I should have been more coy. "Why do you ask?"

He held out a white envelope. "This is for you."

I clutched my keys in my hand, with the sharp point facing outward. "What is it?"

He waved it a little, but I still didn't take it. "I don't know what it says, but my best guess would be that it's a letter."

"Who from?"

His professional facade slipped enough for me to see he was getting irritated with my suspicion. Which only made me more suspicious. "Read it and you'll know."

I smiled because I knew it was crazy before I said it. "What if it's a bomb?"

A slight grin edged his lips upward. "Do I look like a kamikaze limo driver to you? Would I hand you a letter bomb to open three feet away from me?"

I grimaced and took the envelope. "I guess not."

My hands trembled as I slid my finger under the flap and tugged it open. I pulled the folded letter out and looked at the chauffeur. "It didn't blow up."

He tapped his fingers on the steering wheel. "I noticed that."

I unfolded it and gasped. The letterhead read, ALEX CAMPBELL, ATTORNEY-AT-LAW, followed by his address and phone number. The handwritten note was short:

Hey, Water Girl,
   Get in the limo and see what happens.
Trust me?

                              — Alex

My heart slammed against my rib cage. In spite of the hot sun, I shivered. I knew this note was from Alex. Besides the obvious, his letterhead, he wouldn't divulge his crazy nickname for me even under torture. And as far as the "Trust me?" that's my favorite line from my favorite Disney movie, *Aladdin.* When they were about to be caught by the guards, Aladdin held his hand out to Jasmine and said, "Trust me?" and she took his hand. Later, she recognized him when he was disguised as a prince because he said it again — "Trust me?"

Alex knew these things about me. Things no one else did. And the truth was, I did trust him. Totally.

I started toward the backseat door of the limo, but before I could reach it, the chauffeur jumped out and opened it. I climbed in and forced down a giggle. At least he didn't bow.

He closed the door behind me. Just as we eased away from the curb, Lisa and Gail walked out. What would they think about my car still being here? I quickly rolled the window down and waved. "I'll get my car later," I called, feeling "hick" as Lisa would say, but not caring.

They gaped at me, and Gail nodded.

I hit the button to roll the window back up as we pulled out of the parking lot onto the road. I glanced over at the seat next to me and there was a piece of paper with a single word printed on it. *Relax.*

I laughed out loud, even though no one could hear me, then settled back against the leather seat and let the cool air blow gently on my face. So this was luxury. Not bad, but more than anything I couldn't wait to see where we were going.

Out the window, familiar scenery flew by. No surprise that we were going into Lake View. But when we turned down my street, I was surprised. I guess I never thought about a limo just taking someone home. At least not without taking them to an event first.

As we pulled up in my driveway, the partition between me and the driver slowly descended. "I'm to wait here while you get ready." He held up a paperback book. "Take your time."

"Ready for what? How am I supposed to dress?"

"Comfortably."

I met his gaze in the rearview mirror. "Did you make that up, or were you told to say that if I asked?"

"That's what I was told to say." He glanced around as if making sure no one could hear. "My wife said if she was you, she'd dress like she was going to an outdoor barbecue at the governor's house," he said over his shoulder.

I grinned at him in the mirror. "You told your wife about this?"

He ducked his head. "Not your name or anything. Just about the plan."

"The plan?"

He zipped his lip with his forefinger and thumb then got out and opened my door. "Take your time."

"Tell your wife I said thank you." I clutched the letter in my hand and ran up to the door. As soon as I got in, Mr. Persi crowded against me. I patted his head and waved at Neuro up on the couch arm. She blinked her sleepy eyes at me. I called Alex. He didn't pick up. I hadn't really expected him to. I punched in Carly's number on my way to the back door to let Mr. Persi out. Thankfully she answered.

"Carly. Quick. What would I wear to an outdoor barbecue at the governor's mansion?" I let Mr. Persi out and watched him run around.

"You're going to the governor's mansion?"

"No." Gulp. "At least I don't think so."

"What does that mean?"

I held the door open for Mr. Persi to come in then locked it behind him. "Can you come over?" I asked as I walked into my bedroom.

"Now?"

I threw myself backward on the bed. "Please."

"I'll be right there."

I took a shower while I was waiting, towel-dried my long red curls, and threw on an old T-shirt and shorts. When the doorbell rang, I ran down the hall and opened it.

"I wouldn't wear that to the governor's mansion even if I didn't like him," Carly said, apparently by way of greeting.

"Thanks for your valuable fashion advice." I grabbed her arm and pulled her into the house.

She hitched a thumb over her shoulder. "What's the limo doing here?"

I showed her the letter and told her what little details I knew.

She reread the short note. "Wow. This is romantic. Are you sure it's Alex?"

I punched her on the shoulder. Even though I'd asked myself the same thing more than once since this adventure started.

She rubbed her arm. "What? I just asked a simple question."

"Yes, I'm sure it's Alex. Now come help me find something to wear. It's getting dark, and if this plan was for something outdoors, I'm pretty sure I'm late."

"Alex knows what he's doing, I'm sure. So don't worry your pretty little head about it."

I laughed. "You're a very funny girl."

"Thanks, sugar. I try." She pushed me into my walk-in closet. "Now let's get you ready to meet the governor."

"Cracking me up here."

She snatched a pair of flared denim capris off the hanger and laid out a red top and a white short jacket. "It's almost the Fourth of July. Why not go patriotic?"

I considered the outfit then shook my head. "I'm pretty sure I'm not really meeting the governor."

"You're right." She hung the jacket and top up but kept the capris. She added a light green long tank with a brighter green polo shirt over it. With a quick swoop, she snatched my green sandals from my shoe rack and put them with the clothes. "Perfect."

She was right.

When I came out wearing the outfit, she whistled. "I have great taste."

"And such modesty."

She handed me a necklace and earrings. "Just to dress it up a little."

I lifted my hair, and she moved around behind me to fasten the silver chain. As she worked on the clasp, I quickly slipped the small silver hoops into my ears.

Carly circled me as if I were a prize cow at the county fair. "Wonderful. Now turn around."

"Bossy, aren't we?"

She quickly swirled my hair up and secured it with a set of chopstick-style hair sticks.

"What kind of hairstyle is that?"

"It's called a messy bun."

I eyed it in the mirror. "I can see why." The effect was odd but not awful.

"It makes you look casually elegant. Like Cinderella going to the ball."

"In denim capris?"

"It's all in the accessories. And the attitude."

I grinned and hugged her. "Thanks for being my fairy godmother."

"I wouldn't have missed it for the world. Now let's get going before your carriage turns into a pumpkin." She hooked her arm in mine and walked me down the hall. "You'd better call me when you get home tonight. Oh, and before I forget. If you're up for it, ask the prince if he wants to play tennis with Elliott and me tomorrow morning."

"I'd love to. And I'll ask. But you know how much he's been working. I can't believe he's taken time off to plan something like this . . ."

She laughed. "This whatever-it-is?"

"Exactly."

# 17

For wisdom is more precious than rubies,
and nothing you desire can compare
with her.

PROVERBS 8:11

By the time I got back to the limo, it was
dark. I couldn't help but be concerned. I'd
taken less than an hour to get ready, but
what if Alex had something planned that
required daylight? I guess then he would
have instructed me to hurry. So I would just
do what the note said and trust him.

"I think my wife gave good advice and you
followed it well," the chauffeur said as he
held the door open for me to get in.

"Don't forget to tell her I said thanks."

"I already did." He adjusted his hat and
pulled his cell phone half out of his shirt
pocket then dropped it back. "She wanted a
play-by-play of my part in this . . . plan.
Hope you don't mind."

I laughed. "Not at all." I thought back to Alex falling asleep on my couch during the movie last Friday night. I really didn't mind. And I loved that he was comfortable enough with me to do that. But who would have thought then that our romance would be worthy of a play-by-play?

I didn't even try to relax as the limo turned off my street onto the main highway. I tapped on the partition. It slowly lowered.

I smiled at the driver in the mirror. "Do you mind me asking your name?"

He didn't look at me. "You can call me James."

"As in 'Home, James'?"

He chuckled. "I'm Trevor."

"That I believe. Trevor, where are we going?"

"You *are* curious, aren't you?"

"Alex told you I was curious?"

The partition started to slowly rise.

"Or did he say nosy?" I flounced back against the leather seat. My pouty reflection in the window caught my eye and I started to laugh. I didn't even really care where we were going as long as Alex was at the end of the journey.

When we started winding around the lake road, I shook my head. There was no place to go out here. Was he taking me to the lake in a limo? I looked down at my outfit. Even in denim, I was overdressed for a fishing trip. As the limo eased into the marina's parking lot, I reached up to slip off the earrings and necklace. But just when he pulled sideways at the end of the dock, I dropped my hand to my lap and stared down the plank walkway. Tiny white lights outlined the small pavilion at the end of the walkway. And a few brighter lights illuminated the inside of the wooden structure. I opened my door and stepped out as Trevor was getting out of his seat.

He grabbed the handle and bowed low. "Good evening, mademoiselle."

I gave him my sauciest grin. "It sure is." I took a few steps onto the wooden planks and turned back. "Is that a waiter?" I whispered.

He shrugged and shooed me forward.

I tiptoed toward the bright lights.

A wooden podium stood at the entrance of the oblong pavilion, and behind it was a tuxedo-clad man with a napkin across his arm.

When I reached him, he bowed. "This way, please."

"Wait."

He stopped and looked at me. But I had

to have time to gawk. To the left, inside an open booth with counters on all four sides, a man and a woman dressed in white and wearing chef's hats were working furiously. Before I could see what they were working on, the waiter positioned himself between me and them.

"I told you she was curious," a deep voice said from behind me.

I spun around just as Alex stepped out of the shadows. He looked fantastic in jeans and a blue shirt that just matched his eyes. And his slow grin. The one that still made my knees go weak even after all these years of knowing him.

The waiter discreetly stepped away, and in a few seconds, muted classical music filled the air.

Suddenly I felt shy and unsure. "Hi."

"Hi." He stepped toward me, and I instinctively took a step back.

He held out his hand. "Trust me?"

"What?"

"Trust me?"

I put my hand in his. "Totally."

He pulled me close. "You look beautiful," he whispered in my ear.

"Thank you. For all of this," I whispered back.

"Thank you for trusting me and going

along with this." He kissed me on the cheek and released me. "I hope you're hungry."

I put my hand on my stomach. "I think I have too many butterflies to eat."

He laughed. "I knew the curiosity would drive you crazy. But now that you're here, you'll be fine. Let's sit down."

He led me to the table covered with a delicately filigreed white cloth. A bud vase with a single red rose was in the middle. Alex held my chair for me then sat down beside me. Within seconds, the waiter set a crisp green salad in front of each of us then disappeared again.

"Let's pray," Alex said simply.

I bowed and he gave thanks for the food. And for me.

When he finished I met his gaze. "Thank you."

He shrugged. "I thank God for you every day, Jenna."

Soft music filled the silence. I closed my eyes and swallowed against the lump in my throat. It had been a crazy few weeks. And for tonight at least, it seemed like everything had finally fallen into place.

He covered my cold hand with his warm one. "Relax and enjoy tonight. I wanted everything to be perfect, but I didn't mean for you to be nervous."

Me? Nervous? Just because any lingering objectivity I'd had about him was being whisked away with the warm summer breeze? Just because I was being forced to admit to myself that I'd fallen deeply and irrevocably in love with a man who may or may not love me back? Nah. No nerves here. I nodded. "I know. I'm having fun."

"Let's just pretend we're at the diner," he said.

I laughed. "So that's Harvey and Alice over there getting food ready?"

"Yep."

I nodded toward the waiter. "And this is Debbie?"

He leaned forward. "I wouldn't call him that to his face if I were you."

"I'll keep that in mind."

"The fettuccine Alfredo was amazing." I dropped my fork on the empty plate and sat back with a sigh.

"Does that sigh mean you want to take dessert to go?"

"Sure. We can take it back to my house and watch a movie."

He ran his thumb over the back of my hand. "Do you have your heart set on a movie?"

I grinned. "Definitely not. But let's face

it." I waved my arms toward the pavilion extraordinaire. "Anything is going to seem like a letdown after this."

He pulled me to my feet and into the shadows. "Even a trip around the lake to look at the stars?" He pointed to a pontoon boat tethered to the dock.

"Really?"

"The cheesecake is already on board."

I cut my gaze to him. "Race ya." I took off like a shot. Within seconds I could hear his feet right behind me, slapping against the wooden planks. I laughed and ran harder. Just as I jumped onto the boat, he caught me, and we collapsed onto the back bench seat together, laughing. His face was inches from mine and the laughter died on my lips. He stared into my eyes for a long moment, then gently kissed me on the forehead and stood.

I twisted sideways on the seat, with my back to him, and looked out at the dark water, while he started the engine and puttered us away from the dock. If this had been a scene in a movie, it would have ended in a romantic kiss. Not a brotherly peck on the forehead.

Had Alex planned tonight as a way of letting me down easy? Tears stung my eyes. I closed them and let the lake breeze cool my hot cheeks. He drove without speaking. When I felt the engine slow, I sat up just as he pulled into a small cove and killed the motor.

"Are we going to put down anchor?" My voice sounded husky.

He nodded. "Drifting isn't as much fun as it sounds."

I shivered. Was it my imagination, or were we not talking about boating anymore?

The boat rocked as he stepped to the front and flipped up the bench seat to retrieve the anchor. Once it was in place, he came back and sat by me. I was still turned sideways, and he tugged me gently around to face him. "Hey. You okay?"

*Define* okay. I nodded and stared up at the stars. "The stars are beautiful."

"Yet you still manage to put them to shame."

I jerked my gaze back to his face. In the shadow of the running lights, I couldn't see his eyes clearly. But he reached up and cupped my cheek. "I'm sorry."

*Sorry? Sorry for how you've been acting, or sorry for what you're about to say?* I felt sure he could hear my heart beating out a skittish but loud rhythm in the quiet of the night. "Sorry for what?"

"For making things so difficult."

I pressed my hand to my stomach. "Alex, for a lawyer, you're not getting your point across very well. What are you trying to say?"

He dropped his arm around my shoulders and rested his head against the seat. We sat in silence for a few seconds, looking up at the stars. "Last Sunday at the diner . . . when you were with that cop . . ."

"I wasn't —" I couldn't believe that jealousy had been the motive behind this wonderful night.

He leaned up slightly and put his finger against my lips. "Shh. I know. You weren't *with* him. And before you think all this tonight was brought on by jealousy . . ."

I smiled. When did he start reading my mind?

"When you introduced me to him as your friend, I wanted to correct you. But I knew I had no right."

"You could have."

"I know. But what could I have said? That I wanted you to be more than my friend, but I was trying to get my practice up and running before I told you, so keep it hush-hush."

I blew out an exasperated breath. "I don't care about your practice — Wait. That didn't come out right."

"I know what you mean. And ever since you told him I was your friend, I've been rethinking my plan."

"Really?"

He sat up and ran his hand through his hair. I sat up, too, because the whole relaxed-and-looking-at-the-stars thing had just been a front for me anyway.

"When I was fifteen and you were thirteen, you and I went fishing in my little johnboat. In this very cove, actually."

"Really?" We'd fished a lot, but how could he remember what cove we'd been in? And this was an odd time for a fish story.

"You snagged a big trout that day." He pulled his arm out from around me and held his hands out to show the size. "When you pulled it out of the water, you jumped up and almost turned the boat over. You were laughing and your face just glowed. I looked at you and thought, *I'll never love anyone else like I love her.*"

My breath caught in my throat. "Oh."

"And I was right."

"Really?" What a stupid word. But the only thing I could seem to say.

He touched my cheek with his thumb. "You're crying."

*Really?* I didn't say it at least. But I thought it.

274

"You may not feel the same way I do," he said softly. "But I'm in love with you. And I always will be."

"Me, too." I shook my head. "I mean —"

He interrupted me. But not with a brotherly peck on the forehead. This was an "I'll love you forever" kind of kiss.

The next few days flew by in a blur. Tennis with Carly and Elliott, Sunday dinner at Mama's with Alex by my side. Then visiting Reagan in the hospital and working.

We didn't tell anyone about our new commitment, but Mama pulled me over to the side and congratulated me. I joked about her best wishes being premature, but the truth was, I knew it was just a matter of time now. And not too much time.

Tuesday afternoon, I was at my desk writing out a last-minute reminder list for Lisa when Amelia popped her head into my office. "You're taking more vacation days?"

I nodded. "Just for three days, though. I'll be back before you know it."

"That's what you said last time and look what happened."

I looked back at the list. "Barring murder," I clarified, "I'll be back at work Monday."

"Oh, don't even say that. Byron and I are coming up for the tribute concert, and we don't need that kind of excitement." She floated over to the mirror on my wall and tilted her head as if examining her face from every angle. Apparently deciding there were no bad angles, she nodded to herself. "Not that we're likely to get it with the murderer in jail."

I made a noncommittal sound. If only I could believe that. I'd rest a lot easier at night.

"Speaking of that, I guess you don't really need this information anymore, but I found out about Cecil."

I'd planned to corner Ruth and force her to tell me his whereabouts as soon as we got to Branson. This was much easier. "Might as well tell me," I said casually as I stood to make copies of the to-do list. I'd put one in every room and maybe Lisa would actually read one. "Where is he?"

Amelia smiled at me coyly in the mirror. "Well, the good Lord's the only one who knows that." She turned around to face me. "Cecil's dead. And has been for years."

I sank onto my chair. "Are you sure?"

"Absolutely. I knew it myself, really, but I'd forgotten. Why did you want to know?"

"Just curious. Thanks for telling me."

As soon as she was gone, I called Carly. "Mark Cecil off the list. He's dead."

She gasped. "Then who's CeeCee?"

"Who knows?"

"I'm glad you called. Marta wanted to know if Reagan could ride back to Branson with us. Is that okay with you?"

"Sure. Will she get out of the hospital in the morning? When I was there last night, she wasn't sure."

Carly cleared her throat. "Actually she's getting out this afternoon."

"And you think I should invite her to spend the night at my house?"

She laughed. "That's up to you. But I figured you would."

"It's weird how protective I feel about her considering how hard she was to take when we first met her." Visiting her at the hospital every day had made me realize more and more how young and vulnerable she was behind that pretense of sophistication and toughness.

"Not really. A lot of the time when you get to know someone, they're different on the inside than they seem to be."

"Good point, oh wise one."

She sighed. "Just thinking about Holly, I guess, and wondering if there was more I could have done to help her."

"You did all you could, Carly. But I'll call Reagan right now and ask her to stay at my house tonight and ride to Branson with us tomorrow." As far as Holly, I didn't say it, but I did intend to do one more thing for her — find out who really killed her.

# 18

He who trusts in himself is a fool, but he who walks in wisdom is kept safe.
PROVERBS 28:26

"On the road again," Carly sang from the backseat.

"Mom," all three of her kids protested.

Beside me in the passenger seat, Reagan smiled.

"You may wish you'd taken a cab," I joked.

She shook her head. "I appreciate you inviting me. This is much more fun than a long cab ride alone. And thanks again for letting me stay at your house last night. You didn't have to do that."

"I wanted to. And Marta seemed anxious to get you back to the Paradise."

A smile lit her face again. "She offered me a permanent job there, singing on the nights they don't have big names. And opening for the headliners when they are there."

"Wow," Carly said, leaning forward. "That's great. Is that what you want to do?"

"Definitely." She turned to look at Carly. "I don't know if you know, but I'm trying to get started as a songwriter. So being around stars gives me the perfect opportunity for them to hear my stuff and maybe record some of it."

I kept my eyes on the road. "Did Holly listen to your songs?"

She turned her head toward the window and for a few seconds didn't speak. "Yes. She even sang a few of them in her concerts. But she never went through with recording them."

"That must have left you sort of in limbo," I guessed.

She looked at me, and I glanced at her quickly. Her face was bright red. "You might as well know. That day you caught me in Holly's dressing room, I was looking for the CD I'd given her that had my songs on it."

If she was telling the truth, that was one mystery solved. And my gut instinct said she was. Of course, the same gut had thought a dead man was a main suspect, so I wasn't sure. "Did you find it?"

"Yes. Just before you came in. I jumped in the closet and stuffed the CD in the waistband of my jeans." Her voice was so soft I could barely make out her words, and in the mirror, I could see Carly straining against her seat belt to hear. "I'm sorry."

I shrugged with my hands on the steering wheel. "I wasn't supposed to be in there either."

"What were you looking for?"

"I don't know, really. Clues to who killed Holly maybe."

She nodded and looked out the window again. "I'm just glad they caught the killer."

My eyes met Carly's in the mirror. Wouldn't our lives be simpler if we believed that?

She nodded as if in agreement with my unspoken words.

When we pulled into the Paradise breezeway, Dani and Marta were waiting. Carly jumped out and got the crutches from the back, and she and Marta helped Reagan into the building.

"Looks like it's up to us to get the luggage, kiddos," I said.

Dani helped and the five of us loaded everything onto a cart. In the lobby, Ruth and Maurice were at the desk.

Ruth hurried over to me. "I need to talk to you."

Déjà vu. "What's wrong?"

She took my elbow and guided me away

from everyone else. "You and I both know that stalker didn't kill Holly."

"How do you know?"

She frowned. "Because Buck did. He was embezzling from her and he killed her." She looked over at Reagan, who was talking to Marta and Carly. "I'm not sure if Little Miss there knew about it or if she's just guilty of keeping bad company."

Wow. She'd toned down her opinion of Reagan considerably.

"Joey thinks she's innocent. As far as murder goes, at least." Oh, that explained a lot. "I'm not so sure. But either way, I know Buck did it." Maurice waved two room keys at her, and she smiled at him. "We'll talk later," she said from the corner of her mouth.

I nodded, but she was already gone.

"Later" turned out to be about a couple hours later. A knock sounded on our suite door, and when I opened it, Ruth stood there. "May I come in?"

I glanced over my shoulder at the deserted suite. Carly and the kids had gone down to John and Marta's, and I'd hoped to get my Dear Pru letters done and e-mailed so I could join them. "Sure."

Had she watched until the others left? As she walked in, I slid my cell phone off the desk into my pocket. My past experiences had left me a little leery of being alone with people who were possible murder suspects. No matter how innocent they seemed. Appearances could be deceptive.

I motioned toward the couch. "Have a seat."

"You have to help me." She sank onto the sofa.

I sat on the chair across from her. "How can I help?"

"You have to talk to the detective and see why he hasn't at least arrested Buck for embezzlement."

"Detective Jamison?"

She nodded. "I can't talk to him since he arrested Joey like he did. He thinks I'm a crazy old woman."

"Maybe if Maurice went down and told him —"

She held up her hand. "Maurice thinks I should mind my own business and let the police handle it."

"Well, maybe —"

"No!" Tears poured onto her cheeks. "Don't even say he's right. You have no idea what I've been through."

"I know it's been hard with Holly . . . and then with Joey getting arrested."

She covered her mouth with her trembling

hand and shook her head. "That poor boy. Having the past all dredged up like that."

"The past?" I snagged a tissue from the box on the table and handed it to her.

She took it and vigorously blew her nose. I handed her a second tissue. "Thank you."

"The police thought Joey killed Holly because of his dad?" I said as gently as I could.

"Well, because of the accident."

"Accident?"

She twisted the tissues in her hands. "Joey came home from school one day and found Cecil —" Her voice broke and she began to sob.

I moved over by her and put my arm around her, mentally filling in the blank. *With Holly? Dead?*

"— beating me. He was about to kill me." She looked up at me as if to be sure I believed her. "Really."

I patted her shoulder. "I'm sorry."

She stared at the blank TV as if seeing the scene playing there. "Joey ran at him and shoved him. Cecil was three sheets to the wind anyway. He toppled forward and hit his head on the fireplace hearth."

"We called 911. But by the time they got there, he was dead."

"Was Joey charged?"

284

"Our lawyer had him plead guilty to involuntary manslaughter so he wouldn't have to do but a few months in juvie." She shook her head. "I wish I'd never gone along with that. It was just an accident." She pushed to her feet.

I followed suit. "That must have been awful, Ruth."

"I didn't mean to dump all this on you. I just need you to talk to the detective and ask him about the bank statements."

After our last phone conversation, the last thing I wanted to do was talk to Detective Jamison. Especially to try again to convince him he had the wrong man. But I couldn't say no to Ruth. "I'll try."

"Thank you." She hugged me and left.

Carly and I didn't get a chance to talk alone until bedtime. I filled her in on everything Ruth said.

Her brows drew together. "So do you think Joey did it?"

"Based on him accidentally killing his father when he was a teen? No." Not that I was ready to cross him off the list.

"But you only have his mother's word that it was an accident. What's she going to say?"

I grinned. "Spoken like a true mother. But you're right. And I think if the stalker hadn't shot Reagan, Joey would probably be going to trial for killing Holly right now. So he should be our main suspect."

"He 'should,' but I get the feeling you're not convinced."

"Everything doesn't add up."

"Speaking of not adding up, are you going to ask Detective Jamison about Buck embezzling?"

"Since Marta has the pool ready, I probably won't even see him while we're here. So I'd have to call him. But I might. We'll see what tomorrow brings."

The wail of an ambulance siren woke me.

Carly stumbled into my bedroom. "I just talked to Marta. Ruth overdosed."

"Is she . . ."

Carly shook her head. "Her pulse is thready, but she has one."

I grabbed my clothes and hurried to the bathroom. Within five minutes, Carly and I were on our way down the hall.

Marta met us. "They just took her in the ambulance. I woke Maurice up and he went with her."

"Why would she do this now?" I asked.

Carly gave me a look I couldn't read.

Marta frowned. "I don't know. She's been talking about starting the museum for

Holly. And she actually seemed excited about it." She put her hands on her hips. "Do you think the Paradise is doomed to tragedy?"

Carly and I laughed.

"Marta, our God is bigger than any jinx, so no, I don't," Carly said firmly.

Marta gave us a sheepish grin. "I know you're right. I'd better go tell John what's going on. Since you're up anyway, you might as well get some breakfast while it's fresh."

After she left, Carly nodded toward the breakfast area with its continental spread. "I guess she's right. You hungry?"

"Not that much. But this way we can talk without waking the kids."

We each filled a plate and made our way over to the booth in the corner. "It seems like a year ago when they questioned everyone in this room," she said as we sat down.

"Yeah, a lot has happened. What was that look about awhile ago? When I asked why Ruth would do this now." I took a bite of an orange slice.

Carly picked at a strawberry. "I was just thinking if she killed Holly it could be remorse. Or if she knew that Joey did it, it could be . . . that." She shivered. "That would be terrible."

"Oh, I didn't even think of that. You're right." I pushed my plate slightly away. "I'm not hungry."

"I know. Me either. If you want me to, I'll swim with you; then maybe we'll feel more like helping Marta."

"Great."


By late afternoon, Carly turned to me. "I've made a hundred phone calls today, making sure everyone knows the details about the concert. But every time I use the phone, I think I should call and check on Ruth."

I nodded. "Me, too."

She grabbed a phone book and looked up the hospital number. I waited while she asked for Ruth's room. "It's ringing," she mouthed.

"Ruth? It's Carly. I thought Maurice would answer."

She frowned. "You're by yourself? Oh."

She mouthed to me. "A nurse is with her."

I nodded.

Carly didn't speak for a few minutes, and I could hear Ruth's excited voice, even though I couldn't tell what she was saying. "Oh, dear. Would you like for me to come over?"

Apparently Ruth said yes, because Carly ended with, "I'll be right over then. 'Bye."

When she closed the phone, she shook her head. "Ruth says she didn't overdose. Someone tried to kill her."

"Do you believe her?"

Carly shrugged, tears glistening in her eyes. "I don't know. But I'm going over there. Will you keep an eye on the twins? Zac and Dani are going to the mall."

"Sure."

The twins ate Happy Meals while I went over Ruth's accusation in my mind. According to Marta, Buck had gotten into town last night. So he had slipped into Ruth's suite and . . . what? Poisoned her sleeping pills? Switched them out for stronger ones?

I tried to wrap my mind around the possibility that Joey had tried to kill his own mother. I wasn't naive enough to think it had never been done. Maybe he was still angry that she let him go to juvie for a crime he didn't commit. Or did commit. Depending on whether Ruth was telling the truth. Of course, if Ruth was lying . . . I swirled a french fry in ketchup.

"Aunt Jenna!"

I looked up.

Rachel pointed at the blob of ketchup I'd squirted onto my sandwich paper. I'd swirled it all over the place. "Oops." I gave the girls a sheepish grin. "I got distracted."

"Distracted enough to get us a hot fudge sundae?" The mischievous glint in Hayley's eyes made me suspicious.

"I'm not sure."

"Mom gets us hot fudge sundaes all the time," she assured me, an impish grin lighting her pixie face.

"Yeah, even when we're full. She makes us eat them." Rachel jerked away as Hayley nudged her. "Well, she does get them for us."

I pulled out my cell phone. "It's too close to your bedtime for me to decide. I'll just call your mom." I wanted to check on Ruth anyway.

Carly answered on the first ring. "Hello," she whispered.

"I take it you're still inside the hospital."

"Yes," she hissed.

"I don't think they'll care that you're on your cell phone. Was there a sign?"

"I didn't see one."

"Then how's Ruth? Tell her I said hi."

I heard her passing on my message. "She says 'hi' to you, too."

More muted talking between them.

"Jenna, she's worried about the embezzlement investigation of Buck. Would you mind calling Detective Jamison?" She lowered her voice, and I could envision her turning away from the bed. "To put her mind at ease. Please."

Why hadn't I just said yes to the hot fudge sundaes? "Okay. I'll call him. And can you find out —"

"Thanks. Oh, someone's calling on the room phone. See you in a little while."

"Wait. The kids want — Carly? Carly?" She'd hung up on me. I'd wanted to know exactly how someone supposedly tried to kill Ruth. I flipped the phone shut. "Hot fudge sundaes all around."

Hayley and Rachel squealed and bounced up and down.

Twenty minutes later, we were happily finishing our sundaes. "Do you think Zac and Dani are on a date?" Hayley asked as she licked ice cream off her spoon.

I froze midbite.

"No!" Rachel looked up at me, her eyes speculative. "Are they?"

"I have no idea," I blurted. When I'd heard the teens were going to the mall, I just figured it was more of the same hanging out they'd been doing the past few weeks. Now that I thought about it, there had been more teasing (Zac) and giggling (Dani) since we got back from Lake View. How could I have not seen what was right in front of my face?

Hayley set her empty sundae cup down. "Didn't Mom tell you to call him? Maybe she's afraid they're kissing."

"She didn't tell me to call him."

"You said 'Okay. I'll call him.' " Rachel did a perfect imitation of me right down to the overburdened sigh.

"Oh, that was someone else. But I'd better call him, too." I hadn't done anything wrong with Detective Jamison, but knowing he'd been interested in me for more than a friend made me feel guilty. Crazy, but my mind doesn't always work logically. "Let's walk while I talk. Your mom will be home before too long."

Out in the parking lot, I fished his card from my cell phone wallet and punched in the number.

"Detective Jamison." His deep voice sounded hurried.

"Hi. It's Jenna Stafford." I guided the kids across the tiny street and over to the Paradise parking area.

"Jenna. It's nice to hear from you."

"Thanks. But I'm calling with a question." The girls were on each side of me, hanging on not only my arms but also my every word. No doubt trying to figure out if this was more than just a business call.

"What can I do for you?"

"Ruth was worried that she'd never heard back from you on those bank statements."

"What bank statements would that be?"

"Holly's."

"I have no idea what you're talking about."

"You know. The ones I found in Buck and Holly's suite right after the murder."

"You *found* them?" The skepticism in his voice made me grit my teeth.

"Yes. Buck asked me to pack up Holly's things."

"Incriminating bank statements and all?" *Call me a liar, why don't you?*

"I'm sure he didn't —" I looked up just in time to see Maurice pull into the hotel lot and park. "You know what, forget it. I've found someone I can ask who won't act like I'm an idiot."

"That car almost ran over us." Hayley pointed dramatically at Maurice's little red car.

"Honey, it didn't even come close." We came up beside Maurice's car. I waved.

He raised his hand in greeting and unfastened his seat belt.

"Not today." Rachel started talking very fast. "The night Miss Holly died. Only nobody cared because she died and we didn't."

"It must have been a different one. He wasn't in town when Miss Holly died."

Why would the detective lie to me about the bank statements? But he must have, because Maurice had specifically said he gave them to "Jamison."

Hayley shook her head. "Well, his car was in town that night. Because it had that funny looking thing on the hood." She pointed toward the dollar sign hood ornament.

Maurice had gotten out of the car with his briefcase and was making his way toward us when everything clicked into place in my mind. The bank statements. The car. Ruth's overdose.

# 19

Do not those who plot evil go astray? But those who plan what is good find love and faithfulness.

PROVERBS 14:22

I stared at him, the color draining from my face. I turned and pushed the kids toward the back entrance of the hotel. Just as I yanked the key card out of my pocket, a hand closed around my arm.

"Going somewhere?"

"We just got back actually. From McDonald's. Wish you'd gotten here sooner. You could have had a hot fudge sundae."

The kids looked at me then at him. He pulled his briefcase away from his body enough for me — and me only — to see the ugly — looking gun aimed at me. "I need to talk to you." His tone was very polite. Innocuous even. I'd been right earlier. Maurice wasn't treating me like I was an idiot.

I nodded and slowly handed the card to Rachel. "You girls go on in. Your mom should be home soon."

"By ourselves?"

I forced a smile. "You can call Marta if you want to. She'll come stay with you until your mom gets home. But I need to go for a ride with Mr. Seaton."

Maurice's eyes flared, and I had a bad feeling I'd pay for that later. But it might save my life if Carly ever realized something was wrong.

"Wear your seat belt, Aunt Jenna." Hayley pointed at Maurice. "He's *not* a very good driver."

He gave her a tight-lipped smile. "You girls run on along. I'll take very good care of your aunt." He guided me toward the car, the gun a very effective prod. "I really shouldn't leave them behind since you told them my name," he muttered close to my ear.

Rachel was just sliding the key into the door slot.

"Please," I murmured, as much a prayer to God as an appeal to Maurice.

"With them along, you might try something heroic. And stupid. It doesn't really matter." He opened the car door for me, and I quickly climbed in.

Within seconds, he was getting in the driver's side. Relief flooded me as the twins made it into the building and the door closed behind them. What did Maurice really know about what I'd figured out?

Maurice drove without speaking. So I figured the proverbial ball was in my court. And if I wanted to stay alive, I needed to keep it bouncing. "I really don't understand why you're taking me. You almost got away with the perfect crime."

He glanced over at me.

"Embezzlement."

He stared straight ahead and pretended I hadn't spoken.

"Since they have Holly's killer in jail, I would have figured you'd just transfer your money to a secure account on a little island somewhere and live out the rest of your days in luxury."

He grunted. Whatever happened to the idea of a talkative killer? The last time I faced a killer, I could barely get a word in edgewise. "Why don't you just tie me up and leave me somewhere?"

He smiled, and it was not a pretty sight. "That's exactly what I have planned, my dear."

Something wasn't right about that, but I pretended to be relieved. "Good."

"You'd do well to remember what happened to Holly when she took me for a fool," he growled.

This couldn't be good. He'd just confessed to murder. Whatever he'd meant by his cryptic answer, I felt certain he didn't intend for me to live through the night.

Back to the ball game. "How did Holly take you for a fool?"

We pulled up to a stop sign. He pressed the gun hard to my side. I stared straight ahead, afraid he'd think I was signaling to the people in the nearby cars. As we slipped out of traffic and turned into a residential section, he relaxed a little. "I made it look like Buck was taking her money. So she asked me to come up Saturday and not tell anyone. Said it was urgent."

I clasped my hand to my mouth, and he jerked the gun. Maurice Seaton. Maurice Seaton. "CeeCee," I breathed. "We thought you were a manicurist."

He looked like he thought I was crazy. "Holly started calling me that when we were first married. I hated it. I told her it sounded like a girl. Which is probably why she did it." He shook his head. "Anyway, she let me in right after the warm-up show started."

That must have been minutes after she pushed Carly and me out of her suite.

"I told her Buck was indeed stealing from her and then mentioned her leaving him."

"So why would you kill her if she believed Buck did it and was leaving him?"

"Shut up." His face turned red, and I thought sure the ball game was over, thanks to my technical foul. I prayed silently, continuing the ongoing plea I'd started when Maurice's hand had first closed over my arm back at the hotel.

He jerked the car into a driveway and leaned over toward me. I flinched, but he just reached overhead to hit an automatic garage door opener.

The little car glided into the garage, and he hit the button again. The door slid closed behind us. My heart, fairly calm before, was slamming against my ribs.

"Get out."

I carefully considered my situation. Expert advice always says don't go with an abductor. But I had to earlier, or he would've hurt the twins. And at this point, what could I gain from bravely proclaiming, "Shoot me now." The longer I dragged this out, the better chance I had of escaping.

He jabbed the gun against my side again. "I said, get out."

I nodded and climbed out of the low car, ever aware of the gun trained on me. He walked around, took my arm, and guided me to a workbench. My gaze followed his hands as he picked up a knife and laid the gun down. Could I grab it? His hard eyes telegraphed the answer — only if I wanted to be filleted like the catch of the day. Just in case, he stayed between me and the gun as he cut a section of heavy-duty string off a roll and tied it tightly around my wrists.

Satisfied I was securely bound, he retrieved the gun and kept it on me while he got his briefcase from the car. Within seconds, we were outside, and he nudged me toward the stairs going down to the lake. The wooden steps creaked loudly in the dusky dark. Down below, water lapped against the dock.

In high school I went through a morbidly romantic Emily Brontë stage. I'd creeped Carly out by telling her I wanted to be in the water when I died. Now that it looked like my wish was about to come true, was it too picky of me to note that I'd meant when I died of old age? I'd envisioned my husband of seventy years carrying me out into the lake and holding me tightly in his arms, the waves sloshing around us as I breathed my last breath.

As we reached the dock, I was tempted to close my eyes and try to pretend I was old and ready to go, but the practical side of me kicked in. Instead I examined everything in the fading light. Was he going to shoot me here and dump me into the lake? If he raised the gun, I'd dive into the water. With my hands tied, swimming would be difficult, but not impossible.

"We're going for a ride," he muttered, shoving me toward a small boat with a big motor. I looked around. Where was everybody? But I couldn't see a soul who would hear me yell for help.

"Don't even think about screaming, unless you'd like to be responsible for innocent lives being lost." He gave me another push.

I fell into the boat, barely catching myself with my tied hands. "But mine is an innocent life."

He snorted. "Your mama should have raised you to mind your own business."

The nerve of him. *My* mama did fine. His mama should have taught him not to kill people.

But he wasn't through. "I never wanted to kill anybody. But even though Holly thought Buck was embezzling from her, she refused to leave him. Then she started making fun of me. Said he might be a crook, but at least he had the guts to go after what he wanted."

"So you killed her?"

He shook his head. "No. I just wanted to show her that she was wrong. So I told her that I was the one who took the money and that I'd made it look like Buck did it." He shoved me to my knees in the bottom of the boat right in front of the driver's chair and pointed the gun at me.

"Then what did she do?" Not that I even cared anymore, but I was desperate to keep the ball moving, anything to avoid that final buzzer.

"She reached for the phone to call the police. If Buck stole from her, she was fine with it. But after all our years together, she was going to turn me in. Send me to prison."

He sat down in the captain's chair facing me. When he didn't immediately start the engine, I realized he was waiting for a response.

"That must have really hurt."

"I'd picked up a guitar string in the hall, just out of habit. I'm kind of a neat freak."

That's not the only kind of freak he was, but I figured I was better off not mentioning that.

"And when she started to call the cops, I just snapped. Before I knew what happened, she was dead." His voice broke. "I loved her."

I couldn't see his face very well in the dark. Was he crying?

"I'm sorry." Believe me, I was so sorry. Sorry that we ever came to the Paradise. Sorry that Holly had reacted like she had. And sorry that I'd let myself get into this situation. I tried to edge closer to him so I could see if his grip on the gun had loosened in his grief.

"Just be still," he barked. All traces of vulnerability were gone from his voice as he started the boat motor. Within seconds, we were zipping through the black water. I couldn't see where we were going. All I could see was where we'd come from. As the lights of his subdivision faded into the distance, my hope grew dimmer, as well.

Tears blurred my vision. The wind whipped my hair forward, and I twisted my body slightly to the side to get it out of my eyes. We were going so fast. If I could somehow throw myself overboard without getting shot, the impact with the water would surely kill me. Despair settled in heavier than the darkness.

*Oh, Lord, please rescue me.*

The boat slowed then stopped. On the shore, a set of bright lights on the bank caught my eye. The campground Alex showed me. I could remember the layout. If

I jumped in the water and followed the North Star, I should come up on the bank at the right place. Unless Maurice shot me here while I still knelt in front of him.

By the glow of the running lights, I could see him as he walked toward me. The boat swayed gently with his steps. "I'm sorry." He put his hand under the string that bound my wrists and pulled me up. My legs prickled pins and needles as they came out of the cramped position.

"I didn't want to kill anyone."

I glared at him, any sympathy I had earlier gone with the feeling in my legs. "You'll never get away with this."

"I already have. That's why I didn't worry about leaving those nosy little twins behind. My plane is fueled and ready at the airport. The money I took from Holly is in an account in the Cayman Islands. In less than an hour, I'll be winging my way to freedom."

Well, pin a medal on him. He was right. And I'd be dead at the bottom of the lake. Unless I acted now. I threw my body weight toward him, being careful not to completely lose my balance. I heard him crash and fumble for his footing, but I scrambled up onto the live well and did my best no-hands dive over the side. It might not qualify for the Olympics, but — The thought was interrupted by a loud explosion. A searing pain hit my left shoulder just as I hit the water. The icy darkness swallowed me. The cold made it hard to think, but it also numbed the pain. Instinct brought me to the surface quickly. A spotlight reflecting off the water near me cleared some of the fog from my brain. I dove deep, counting the cost, but knowing that if I didn't take the chance, I was lost.

I stayed under until I was about to lose consciousness, then kicked my way upward, praying I hadn't gotten turned around. I could be propelling myself to the bottom of the lake. Just as I thought sure I'd gone the wrong way, I broke the surface again. The light was nowhere to be found, and the sound of the boat motor faded into the distance as I treaded water, using my bound hands as one large fin.

Choppy waves were all I could see, so I braced myself and bounced out of the water, using my feet to shoot me up. "Oww!" The intense pain made my head spin. Spots in front of my eyes replaced the night sky. "If I faint, I die," I said to the water. I bounced up one more time, not as vigorously. The lights of the campground weren't too far. At least not too far if my hands weren't tied and I weren't possibly dying from a gunshot wound. I couldn't keep bouncing, so I looked up and thanked God for the cloudless night. The North Star shone right over the campground. I swam toward it, pushing through the pain like I used to when I was in training. Not that the coach shot me back then.

My mind was seriously starting to jumble. I began to count the strokes silently. *One. Two. Three. Go toward the star. Four. Five. Six. Three. No. Wait. Go toward the star.* Finally I just switched to *Star. Star. Star. Star. Star. Star.* With each word, I pulled water toward me with my bound hands and kicked, sort of a variation of the frog stroke I used to do when I was tiny. I kept my focus on the star and let it guide me. But finally I knew I was beat. I couldn't swim anymore. I stopped and my feet grazed against something. I tentatively reached down with my toes and then let my weight rest on solid ground.

*Thank You, thank You, thank You, God.*

The tears started to flow, and by the time I got to the shore, I was on my knees, sobbing great gulping sobs. "Help." I wanted to lay on the rocks and sand until I could quit crying. Until I could think. I barely knew my name. But I did know one thing. Maurice was going to get away if I didn't get help.

That possibility brought me to my feet. "Help." I called louder as I stumbled into the lighted area around the cabins. "Help!"

One porch light clicked on. Then another. A woman came out of the first house, a little girl clutching her leg. Two guys, a few years older than Zac, walked out on the porch of the second.

"You poor thing." The woman rushed over and put her arm around me. "Go get some towels, Lilly."

The guys took a few steps closer and the tallest one peered at me. "You're bleeding."

"Got a pocketknife?" the woman asked him.

He looked at his buddy, who fished in his pocket and pulled out a Swiss army knife. He reached over and cut the twine.

I clutched my left arm against my body.

"Call 911," I croaked out. The tall guy looked a little afraid of me, but he pulled out his cell phone and dialed.

"What should I tell them?" he said.

"Tell them to send an ambulance, you goose," the woman snapped.

"No, wait! I'll talk." I held out my right hand.

"She wants my phone?" he said to his

friend, who shrugged.

The woman yanked the phone from his hand and put it in mine.

When the operator answered, I took a deep breath and tried to ignore the spinning. "This is Jenna Stafford. Get in touch with Detective James . . . Jamison."

"Ms. Stafford, where are you?"

"Tell him Maurice Seaton confessed to killing Holly Wood. He's on his way to the Hollister airport. You have to stop him. Hurry."

"But where are you?"

I told her the campground name then remembered there was one more thing. "Oh. And he shot me."

I don't know what happened to the guy's cell phone when I surrendered to the encroaching blackness and tumbled to the ground.


"Holly would have been so happy."

I smiled at Carly's reflection in the mirror. Her dark curls framed her glowing face. "You look pretty happy yourself. And I don't think it's because of all the stars we're going to see tonight."

She sat down beside me on the vanity bench and absently fluffed her hair. "It's not just because Elliott's here. Although I admit, that is really somethin'. It's also the fact that you're here." She motioned toward the sling that held my arm. "Alive and able to go to the concert. When I heard you'd been shot . . ."

I nodded and leaned forward to touch up my lipstick with my good hand. "It was scary."

"You know, Alex never left your bedside. Even when Mama and Daddy got there, he stepped back but stayed in the room. I think he was afraid to take his eyes off you."

"Probably afraid I'd stumble into another murder." I stuck my lipstick in my purse.

"Very funny. He does worry, but it's because he loves you."

"Yes, he does. Isn't it wonderful?" I knew I sounded like a love-struck idiot, but it was so nice to finally feel that Alex was totally committed to our relationship. "Ready to go watch the concert?"

We met Alex and Elliott in the lobby. As we handed our tickets to the usher, he smiled. "Front row seats. Nice."

"That's what happens when you know the owners," Carly whispered to me. "We shouldn't be mixing Brad Paisley up with the post office guy tonight, that's for sure."

I nodded and waved at Zac and Dani, who were seated midway. Zac blushed a little, and I realized they were holding hands. Guess that explained why they didn't want to sit with the rest of us.

Mama and Daddy along with the twins were seated on the front row with us. Before we even got up there, I could see the twins' bobbing heads. They were thrilled to be seeing so many stars up close and personal. But no more thrilled than the rest of us, probably.

As soon as the performance began, though, there was no doubt that it was a tribute. Even though almost every well-known country music artist appeared on the stage, they selflessly made it all about Holly. In the background the huge screen flashed a silent montage of the Queen of Country Music's concerts as the performers sang her greatest hits and told touching stories about her. Before the night was over, I decided Carly might have been right. There could have been more depth to her than I realized.

When it was over, the crowd went wild. As the cheering and clapping showed no signs of stopping, I glanced over at Carly, who had tears streaming down her cheeks.

I leaned over to speak into her ear. "Holly would have been happy. Even though she was far from perfect, she touched a lot of lives for good."

She squeezed my hand and nodded.

Later, after the stage lights were down and the auditorium was empty, we went backstage to say good-bye to everyone.

Ruth hugged us both. "I've decided to buy the land next door for Holly's museum."

"Here in Branson? Next to the Paradise?" Marta would be thrilled.

Ruth nodded. "It's only fitting. I've been on the phone all afternoon trying to get things ready." She wiped away a tear. "I still can't believe Maurice killed her. He loved her so much."

I hugged her. "I think he did, too, but he just went crazy."

"And to think that he tried to kill me, too. At least running the museum will keep me busy." Ruth twisted the Kleenex in her hand. "Keep my mind occupied."

Just then, Joey came in, loosely supporting Reagan, who was on crutches. Was that compassion on Ruth's face when she looked at Reagan?

Joey hugged his mother. "It turned out really well. Holly would be pleased with what you've done."

I leaned down and hugged Reagan with my good arm. "You take care of yourself. Stay in touch, okay?"

She smiled. "I will."

"Good luck with your new job. We'll be back to hear you sing before too long."

"Thanks." She looked over at Joey. "I'll at least have someone in the house band that I already know."

I smiled at Joey. "Congratulations on your new job, too, then."

To my amazement, he flashed me an almost sunny smile in return. "Thanks."

As they walked away, I felt an arm around my waist, and I looked up into Alex's twinkling eyes. "I think this is the end of the yellow brick road. You sorry it's over?"

I laughed. "It's been an adventure, but I have to say that Dorothy's right. There's no place like home."

# ABOUT THE AUTHORS

Sisters **Christine Pearle Lynxwiler, Jan Pearle Reynolds,** and **Sandy Pearle Gaskin** are usually on the same page. And it's most often a page from their favorite mystery. So when the idea for a Christian cozy mystery series came up during Sunday dinner at Mama's, they determined to take their dream further than just table talk. Thus the Sleuthing Sisters mystery series was born.

**Christine** writes full-time. She and her husband, Kevin, live with their two children in the beautiful Ozark Mountains and enjoy kayaking on the nearby Spring River. **Jan,** part-time writer and full-time office manager, and her husband, Steve, love to spend time with their two adult children and their granddogs on the lake or just relaxing at home. **Sandy,** part-time writer and retired teacher, works with her husband, Bart, managing their manufacturing business.

With their daughter off to college, she hopes to devote more time to writing. The three sisters love to hear from readers by e-mail at sleuthingsisters@yahoo.com.

You may correspond with these authors by writing:
Christine Lynxwiler, Sandy Gaskin, Jan Reynolds
Author Relations
PO Box 721
Uhrichsville, OH 44683